JEWISH VIGNETTES

We Are Personally Involved

Michael B. Grossman

ATHENA PRESS
LONDON

JEWISH VIGNETTES: *We Are Personally Involved*
Copyright © Michael B. Grossman 2002

All Rights Reserved

ISBN 1 932077 47 2

First Published 2002 by
MINERVA PUBLISHING CO.
1001 Brickell Bay Drive, Suite 2310
Miami, Florida 33131

Published 2003 by
ATHENA PRESS
Queen's House, 2 Holly Road
Twickenham TW1 4EG
United Kingdom

Printed for Athena Press

JEWISH VIGNETTES
We Are Personally Involved

ABOUT THE AUTHOR

Michael (Mike) Grossman is the youngest of ten brothers and a younger sister. During World War II, he served in the Navy along with seven brothers who also served in the Armed Forces. Altogether, they participated in thirty-five battles. Mike is a graduate of the University of Pittsburgh as a Metallurgical Engineer. He has been a Registered Professional Engineer in the states of Pennsylvania and California and is in *Who's Who of the West*. He has been President of the David Lubin Lodge of B'nai B'rith in Sacramento (which is 148 years old) in 1997 and 1998, and is now editor of their monthly periodical. He has dedicated a grade school along with a hundred year time capsule. He had served as a Value Engineer for the Air Force (as a civilian) where he saved approximately $4,000,000, and as a Quality Assurance Division Manager. His service for the Air Force exceeded 20 years. He is a resident of the Sacramento area with his wife Sylvia and two children (one a pediatric dentist and the other an oncology patient care coordinator).

Contents

INTRODUCTION

History recounts the rise and fall of one civilization after another. The thread of continuity from one empire to its successor, from the ashes of one to the majesty of another, from the beginning of modern civilization to the present, is the Jewish people. Not the Jewish religion alone, or the acquired customs alone, nor the law (the Torah), that bound their communities together. For one or more of these was dormant at one point or another in history. Wrap these together with a history that is remembered because it is recorded and you have the lasting alloy, the conglomerate that is the Jewish people.

But why do a number of Jews, both adults and youngsters, acknowledge that they are Jews but feel it's no big deal and so, they do not partake in the community or support it? Why do some Jews disappear into the woodwork – their only link being a gastronomic one? "Yesiree, a good corned-beef sandwich, a knish or blintzes hits the spot!" Well, there are several reasons: One of these is understanding what we are "davening" (reading/praying) in the language of the country in which we reside. Oh, they have been taught to read Hebrew but haven't been taught to translate what they are reading. The logic, the beauty, the message, therefore, escapes them. A translation of the Hebrew should be placed alongside or nearby.

Alas, we Jews have not had a semblance of good public relations relative to teaching what our religion stands for. People are looking for heroes, people they can worship, they can aspire to, they can claim kinship to. "Preaching to the choir" does not increase attendance or draw our people out of the woodwork. But letting them know that we have many heroes will change the picture. In every age of civilization, we have had our heroes. Here, our public relations have been negligent – these heroes have only been identified as Spaniards, Germans, English, Americans, etc., but we didn't tell the non-Jews (and Jews) that these men or women were Jews.

That is the reason for this book. History is fascinating when you feel personally involved. Here you will learn about a few of our heroes. A book can probably be written about each one of them, but I have synopsized their lives, careers and exploits. Those of you who are Jewish have a heritage you can be proud of. Experiences of Jews in various countries are also covered here. The origin of Hebrew, Yiddish, the Talmud, and the Kabala are also touched upon.

REDEMPTION

You've all heard about the Southern Baptist's plan to convert Jews to Christians. Besides them, there are the Jews for Jesus, the Hebrew Christians and some evangelical groups. There is a reason they don't try to convert Buddhists, Moslems and others. After all, Christianity was the "successor religion" to Judaism and we Jews are stupid, stubborn and stiff-necked not to realize that. And, of course, Christianity is so wonderful because a goodly portion of the world has embraced it. Also, because we Jews didn't do the right thing by converting, we have been burned at the stake, raped, slaughtered, ghettoized, ostracized, etc., by "honest, God-loving" Christians.

Multitudes of Jews who did not suffer the above fates were forced to convert to save the lives of their families. Those who did not convert lost not only their lives, but also their property and assets. Many converts from Spain and Portugal are today still known as *Conversos* and/or *Marranos* (people who converted under duress). The descendants of the converts practice customs which are of Jewish origin. These converts do not realize their origin, but follow customs practiced by their ancestors, such as – putting stones on grave markers, the bride marching around the groom at the wedding, lighting candles one day of the week, and in some cases, even abstaining from eating pork or shellfish.

A great number of Jews escaped from Spain and Portugal to Turkey, the Middle East, Greece and the New World. At one time, it was estimated that twenty percent of the population of Mexico City was of Converso origin. They populated a number of countries in South America until the Portuguese and Spanish extended the Inquisition to Brazil and Argentina.

Jews do not believe in proselytizing. But, I believe we have a right to redeem those who have been stolen away from us by force. This is not proselytization, it is "redemption". It is estimated that there are at least 1,500 families in New Mexico, of

Marrano origin. There are many Latinos, for example, who fall into this category. According to their last name (apellido), many can be easily identified as descendants of Jews. Herein are listed just a few of these:

Sutra, Peixotto, de Torres, de Calle, Alonzo, de Dios-Porto, Ellis, de Cordova, Sabbatha, Acosta, Delgado, Bravo, Andrade, Morales, Hart, Pereira, Mendes, Diaz, Fernandez, Marcheva, Cohen, de Aranjo, de Yuan, da Costa, Maduro, de Castro, Henrigues, Spinoza and Pinero. The articles herein bear this out – including their history.

In Europe, there were many forced conversions. During World War II, many Jews gave their children to their non-Jewish neighbors in Poland, to save them from slaughter. As a result, nowadays we hear of men and women being told they were Jews. Then they seek information on Judaism and what this could mean to them. The same is true in other countries. In Poland alone, over 4,000 youths have joined Jewish groups. Estimates range up to 20,000 Jews who can realize their true heritage.

So, now is the time to fight back, to reclaim what was once a part of our people, to tell Christians that we will be on the offensive, that we have a religion that is healthy, complete and does not need "miracles" to function. "Redemption" should be our goal.

Chapter I

SOME NOBEL PRIZE RECIPIENTS UP TO 1936

> And I will bless you, and curse him that curses you, and in you shall all the families of the earth be blessed.
>
> Genesis 12:3

That is what God said to Abram (later Abraham), when He asked Abram to leave his home and his land, the city of Haran in Mishpot (Mesopotamia). From a very small percentage of the earth's inhabitants, the Jews, indeed, have been a nation of "priests" unto the world. I use the word "priests" in the context of men who benefit their fellow men. For indeed, one of the measures of a man's contribution to mankind, the Nobel Prize, bears this out. Here are some, not all, of the Jews to receive the Nobel Prize:

Year	Name	Deed or Field
1905	Bayer	Chemistry
1907	Michelson	Physics
1908	Ehrlich	Medicine
1908	Metchnikoff	Medicine
1910	Wallach	Chemistry
1911	Asser	Peace
1911	Fried	Peace
1914	Barany	Medicine
1915	Wilstaetter	Chemistry
1918	Haber	Chemistry
1921	Einstein	Physics
1922	Meyerhoff	Medicine
1925	Hertz	Physics
1928	Bergson	Literature

Year	Name	Deed or Field
1930	Landsteiner	Medicine
1931	Warburg	Medicine
1936	Loewi	Medicine
1936	Ossietsky	Peace

After 1936, there were many more. But let's talk about some who didn't get the Nobel Prize and their contribution to the following actions:

Selman Waksman discovered Streptomycin – used to destroy, to a great extent, Tuberculosis and other diseases.

Joseph Goldberger discovered the prevention and cure of Pellagra.

Jonas Salk and the Staff of University of Pittsburgh discovered polio vaccine.

A. B. Sabin discovered polio vaccine.

Ehrlich (previously mentioned) discovered Salvarsan to fight Syphilis.

Ludwig Trabo discovered Digitalis.

Solomon Stricker discovered Cocaine.

Widall and Weil discovered Typhus.

Minkowsky discovered Insulin.

Sprio and Eiloge discovered Pyramidon and Antipyrin for headaches.

Oscar Leibeich discovered Chloral Hydrate for convulsions.

Sigmund Freud founded Psychoanalysis.

Of course, there are many, many more such men, but I'll venture to state that you hadn't heard about a number of them. They are listed as German, Norwegian, Americans, etc. Why? Because the world believes that "Jewish" means a religion, not a nationality.

Chapter II

THE ASSER LEVY STORY OF CIVIL RIGHTS

The first Jew (on record) arrived in America in 1621. In 1656, services were conducted in Delaware; in Connecticut, in 1659; and in Rhode Island, in 1658. In 1677, the Jews of Rhode Island purchased ground for the first Jewish cemetery in the colonies. The Jews appeared in the Carolinas in 1665, in Virginia in 1700 and 1773 in Georgia. The first Jewish synagogue was built in Newport, Rhode Island in 1668. All these events, however, paled by comparison to the impact that one Jew had on American history and the building of the largest city in the world – New York.

Many Jews had moved to Brazil to escape the Inquisition in Portugal and Spain. In 1631, the Dutch conquered the Pernambuco area of Brazil, which is now Recife. The Marrano Jews, who comprised a significant Jewish community in Brazil, openly returned to Judaism. Unfortunately, Portugal reconquered the area around 1660 and expelled all Jews. A group of thirty Jews, including Asser Levy van Swellem, a "shochet" (ritual slaughterer), landed in the West Indies. They found little comfort there and headed for a Dutch colony, New Amsterdam, because it was surrounded by Protestant States and clear of the torture of the Inquisition. Twenty-three people joined Asser Levy on this trip.

When Peter Stuyvesant, the Dutch governor and a Jew hater, heard that so many Jews wanted to come ashore, he refused them permission to disembark. Levy had powerful friends in Amsterdam and told Stuyvesant so, including the fact that they had come 2,000 miles and would sit all winter in his harbor, aboard ship, if he didn't let them land. Stuyvesant gave in, and they landed. This was the winter of 1653.

In 1654, Stuyvesant ordered all able-bodied men to attack the Swedish colony on the Delaware River. This order, of course, didn't include Jews, but Jews were told to pay a monthly contribution for exemption from the army. Levy refused. Levy fought Stuyvesant on a dozen different occasions in the Town Council, the Courts, etc., and Levy always won. Their feud was famous in Holland also. Levy obtained a butcher's license and acquired two sailing crafts and started trading up the Hudson. Stuyvesant forbade anyone to deal with the Jews, so Levy wrote to Amsterdam. Stuyvesant was rebuked by the New Amsterdam Company back in Holland. Levy got the Jews the right to be butchers. The Dutch people of New Amsterdam loved him because he fought every step of the way. Levy was the first Jewish landowner in New York City, where he opened a Kosher and non-Kosher slaughterhouse.

In 1664, the British took New Amsterdam, but Levy started trading with them also, as in London and Amsterdam. Levy put up the money to build the first Lutheran Church in New York City.

Levy's son settled in Connecticut. His grandson appeared as an officer in the New Jersey regiment during the American Revolution. Levy was loved by all – Gentile and Jew alike. His fight for all Jews was famous in all the seaboard colonies. Because of Levy's deeds, Jews settled in New York by the thousands to build up trade routes, merchant centers and banking houses. The term "a swell", meaning a rich man, is a paraphrase of Asser Levy van Swellem.

Chapter III
REBECCA GRATZ

Rebecca Gratz was one of the most beautiful and gracious women of her time, who devoted her life to charitable causes and to her friends, both famous and common. Born to wealth and high position in Philadelphia in 1781, the decisive year of the Revolutionary War, Rebecca lived to see the Union restored after Lee's surrender at Appomattox.

Among her friends was Washington Irving who, on a visit with Sir Walter Scott in England, told the great author how Rebecca, at the peril of her own life, had nursed Irving's fiancée, the eighteen-year-old Matilda Hoffman, dying from tuberculosis. Scott, never knowing Jews and indulging in the prejudices of the day, was struck with the compassionate Rebecca, and the high esteem in which Philadelphia held the Gratz family. Scott immortalized her as the lovely and faithful Rebecca in his celebrated novel, *Ivanhoe*.

A devout Jew, Rebecca Gratz fell in love with a man not of her faith, Samuel Ewing, son of Dr. John Ewing, noted clergyman and Provost of the University of Pennsylvania. Instead of marriage, she wedded her life to the service of fellow Jews less fortunate than she.

Among Rebecca's charities and the Jewish organizations which she helped to found and worked in were: the Philadelphia Orphans' Home, the Female Hebrew Benevolent Society, the Jewish Foster Home and the Hebrew Sunday School Society of Philadelphia. For many years, she was concerned with the religious training of all Jewish children, including those of her own synagogue. Under her direction, the first Jewish Sunday School in the United States opened in 1838.

Rebecca Gratz was acclaimed as one of the noblest women in the world, when she was laid to rest in Mikvah Israel Cemetery in Philadelphia in 1869 at the age of eighty-eight.

Chapter IV

DEDICATION ADDRESS OF DAVID LUBIN ELEMENTARY SCHOOL

SACRAMENTO, CALIFORNIA
NOVEMBER 5, 1977
MICHAEL GROSSMAN
President of David Lubin Lodge of B'nai B'rith

Ms. Chairperson, Rabbi Frazin, Reverend Chinn, Mr. Vanosek, Staff, Ladies and Gentlemen,

We're all here to honor the memory and achievements of a man of humble beginnings who rose to world prominence. I am proud to be given the honor of saying a few words about that man – David Lubin. What makes me even happier is that we can share this moment with two of David Lubin's grandchildren, Miriam Lubin Powers and Jess Lubin. This school and our B'nai B'rith Lodge bear his name. Just why is David Lubin so famous? Let's recount a little of his life.

David Lubin was born in Lublin, Poland in 1849, in the Jewish "Pale of Settlement", an area where Jews were restricted to live. His family fled to the United States when he was six years old. He became a peddler and sold anything that would sell. When he heard about "gold" in California, he made his way west. When he saw every inch of riverbed covered with miners, he figured there wasn't any room for him! The fact of the matter was there was no room even to swing a pan, so he started peddling again.

He built a reputation as an honest man who charged a fair price. He opened up a store selling pots, pans, clothing – anything that people needed. What's more important, he charged the same price to everyone. He became prosperous and his brother-in-law,

Harry Weinstock, joined the business. David Lubin bought some land and started growing fruit. He knew absolutely nothing about farming at first, but he read everything he could on the subject of agriculture. He started experimenting with cross-fertilization to develop new breeds, finally developing a new strain of wheat. He helped organize the farmers to work together. He pioneered a fruit growers' association to protect the farmers' rights. He became involved in the "cause célèbre" of the time, fighting against the land grabbers, the railroads, financiers and middlemen. Leland Stanford was one of these, as was Crocker. Both men later subsidized the Stanford University and the Crocker Art Gallery, respectively.

By this time Lubin's name was known by farmers all over the world because of the work he had pioneered in agriculture and his fighting on behalf of the farmers. He contacted farmers in many countries in an effort to make a worldwide farmers' organization. He obtained the support of the king of Italy and, in 1905, he founded the International Institute of Agriculture (IIA) in Rome and was elected its president. Forty nations were represented – even nations at war with each other. Lubin worked hard to make the IIA a success. I have here a copy of a lecture given in 1940, by H. G. Wells, the famous science fiction author and orator. He states that David Lubin was one of those visionaries who tried to make a worldwide farmers' organization but it was doomed to a slow death. H. G. Wells was premature in his predictions of the demise of the IIA – it is still in operation and servicing farmers of many nations. The IIA did much to make farming more economical by reducing waste in foodstuffs. As a matter of fact, the International Institute of Agriculture led the way to the establishment of the League of Nations. Now, I am sure you've all heard of the League of Nations.

David Lubin died in 1919. Every civilized county in the world lamented his death. He was buried in Rome and a statue was erected there to commemorate his deeds. The Etham Lodge of B'nai B'rith (established in 1853), of which he was a member, changed its name in 1922, to David Lubin B'nai B'rith. You knew the store he founded as the David Lubin Store, then Weinstock Lubin, then Weinstocks. Here you have a Horatio Alger story of a penniless immigrant who became a worldwide statesman and philanthropist, Sacramento's most noted citizen.

It is for this man that we unite, all the Masonic Lodges of Sacramento, the David Lubin Lodge of B'nai B'rith, Sacramento, the faculty of David Lubin Elementary School, together with the blessings of the Sacramento City School District, and the Governor of the State of California, to dedicate this facility, this house of learning, in the name of David Lubin. I am sure the graduates of this school will go on to honor it. Who knows, but one of its pupils may go on to become the president or to reach posterity in some other field!

Note: Some papers and artifacts were enclosed in a time capsule as part of the building and are scheduled to be opened in a hundred years.

Chapter V
THE HEBREW LANGUAGE

The Jews are very proud of the fact that we have revived an ancient language and made it international, to a great degree. The Irish have tried to revive Gaelic and have failed, along with other modern cultural groups who have tried to revive their ancient languages. In addition to reviving it (it was never really dead), we have modernized it by the addition of thousands of words. There is a body in Israel whose official duty is the "care and feeding" of Ivrit (Hebrew). The language is changing almost daily with the incorporation of new words from old roots, new meanings from old world, additions of foreign words such as penicillin, ottoboos (autobus or bus), machinot (auto or machine), etc.

There are those of us who think we have the oldest language. This, of course is not true. But I'll bet you didn't know that the English alphabet is indirectly derived from the Hebrew. The Jewish Publication Society publishes a very interesting book titled, *The Origin Of Hebrew*, by Professor Chomski. Here we learn some very interesting facts based on intense research, archeological findings and studies of ancient manuscripts.

Where is English related to Hebrew? The English alphabet is derived from the Latin alphabet, which in turn, is derived to a large extent from the Greek alphabet. The Greeks obtained their alphabet from the Phoenician and Jewish sailors who exported it from Israel, Judea and the Levant. The Greeks used to write from left to right and right to left at one time. In an attempt to standardize, they decreed that "left to right" was the standard, and in so doing, turned over some of the Hebrew letters from facing left to facing right. This made it easier to write from left to right. Compare the aleph, bet, gimel, daleth of Ivrit with the alpha, beta, gamma, delta, etc., of the Greek alphabet.

But, let's stop and think. Where did Hebrew derive its

alphabet? Do you remember in Genesis, where Abram (Abraham) left Ur of the Chaldees (now Iraq) to go to Haran with his kinsmen, and then traveled in great numbers westward to Canaan (now Israel and Jordan)? Round about that era, the Assyrians ruled a fairly good-sized empire including Babylonia (now Iraq). The language spoken there was Akkadian (or Assyro-Babylonia). This was considered a forerunner to Hebrew, if not a close relative. It was natural to take your own language with you and change it with time, environment and experience. And so developed Hebrew. Aramaic was also spoken, although believed to have developed the same way and used subsequently, by the whole of Middle East and parts of Mitzraim (Egypt). Aramaic became the vernacular or the common everyday language spoken by the laborer, the merchant and the common folk. It is not considered, if memory serves me, to be as old as Hebrew. Did you know that even today, some of the prayers you recite, including the Kaddish, are in Aramaic, not really Hebrew? Very little noticeable difference to you, isn't that right?

Now, where did Akkadian come from? This is obscure. It is thought that Sanskrit, used in India played a part. It is also thought that the spoken language of an older culture, the Egyptians, played a very prominent part. But the Egyptians didn't really develop a written language, as we knew it then. They used hieroglyphics to depict events and happenings and only wrote foreign words that they added to their culture. Who knows for sure?

Lately (1929), there have been found in Syria, samples of another "forerunner" of Hebrew, thought to be older and of the same type used in the Torah. It is called Ugarit. The poetry, the meter, the idioms, the sayings are found in the Torah also. "As blue as the sky", "The dawn broke" and other sayings were found in these writings.

In conclusion (and I'm adding my own beliefs here now), add Ugarit, Canaanite, Assyro-Babylonian, Aramaic and a tinge of Egyptian and Sanskrit and that equals Hebrew. By the way, Moshe (Moses) and Miriam are Egyptian names. Hasta la vista, arrivederci and shalom.

Chapter VI

JOSEPH SELIGMAN – THE AMERICAN ROTHSCHILD

In the early 1800s, Jews in Germany were restricted economically, politically and socially. They were forced to be peddlers, shop-keepers and moneylenders. They could only own the land where their houses stood in the ghetto. The number of Jewish marriages was restricted to keep the Jewish population small. Jews even had to pay a poll tax each time they left the ghetto to peddle.

Joseph Seligman, one of eight brothers and three sisters, was born in Baiersdorf, Germany in 1819. His father operated a dry goods store selling lace, ribbons, sheets, pillowcases and bolts of cloth. In addition, he had a sideline selling sealing wax. Joseph started in business early at the age of eight years, by starting a money-changing service for travelers, making a small profit on each transaction. By the age of twelve, he operated a miniature American Express Company, learning economics, arithmetic and geography while he practiced his trade.

When Joseph was fourteen years old, his mother enrolled him in the University of Erlangen, using savings she had scraped together. He graduated at the age of sixteen with excellence and gave his farewell oration in Greek. He could speak German, Yiddish, Hebrew, some English, and some French, in addition to Greek. He came home from the university determined to go to America where a Jew could live in dignity.

At the age of seventeen, Joseph and eighteen other Baiersdorf boys climbed aboard a horse-drawn wagon to go to Bremen. During the trip, which took seventeen days, they camped along the road at night. Their passage in steerage class cost forty dollars and included one meal per day consisting of pork, beans and a cup of water. The ship was dark and filthy, and Joseph slept on a wooden plank. The trip took nineteen weeks.

Once in America, he hiked to Mauch Chunk, Pennsylvania, a distance of one hundred miles, where he went to work for Asa Packer, as a cashier clerk for $400 a year. Packer, who in 1837 was a small town prosperous businessman, became a multimillionaire and a congressman (1853–57). He was also the founder of Lehigh University and the president of the Lehigh Valley Railroad. Packer thought a great deal of young Joseph Seligman.

After a year of working for Packer, Joseph started on his own peddling around the farm country. He had made enough money to send for three of his brothers by 1841, and they opened a store in Lancaster, Pennsylvania. Joseph then shaved off his beard and side locks and discarded his black coat and hat for modern clothing. One of his brothers, James, got a horse and went to the South, where he peddled. Soon, the other brothers followed, taking with them $5,000 in merchandise to set up headquarters in Mobile, Alabama. Their success there enabled them to send for the rest of the family.

Joseph's brothers soon had four dry-goods stores in different towns, and eventually, they had a chain of stores stretching as far as St. Louis and New York.

His brother Jesse opened a store in San Francisco in 1850, and due to the "gold fever" and the shortage of goods he was able to get high prices for his merchandise. In 1851, when a fire wiped out most of the city, his store was the only one left. By this time, they were selling pots and pans, whiskey and gold. Dealing in gold bullion soon put them into the banking business in New York.

The Seligmans started business in Pennsylvania in the 1840s, moved south thereafter, and made their headquarters in Mobile, Alabama. Jesse Seligman opened up a store in San Francisco in 1850, taking advantage of the increased demand for goods resulting from the 1849 California Gold Rush. The gold received from selling the scarce goods was sent to New York, where it was used to start the enterprise for which Joseph Seligman and his brothers became famous.

Joseph Seligman found that when you lent out money, it worked for you twenty-four hours a day, not just from 8 A.M. to

5 P.M. as in a store. In 1852, he started trading on the Gold Market in New York. During the panic of 1857, he was "in cash", having heard rumors about the shakiness of certain banks. The Seligmans then bought a factory that produced undershirts and pants. They soon added uniforms for the Union Army.

The United States Government was broke at the start of the Civil War! They paid for some uniforms in cash, then dumped 7.3 per cent bonds on the Seligmans in payment. The Seligmans had to sell these bonds to get cash to stay in business. They were soon selling Union bonds all over Europe. Indeed, they were responsible for financing the Union side of the War. One of their personal friends was General Ulysses S. Grant. Their suggestion to President Lincoln that Grant head the Army was probably one of the factors leading to his appointment.

In 1865, the Seligman brothers sold sixty million dollars of a $400 million issue of new government notes. By the end of the Civil War, the Seligman name was very big in Washington. Joseph then set up the International Banking House of Seligman, a copy of Rothschilds' with offices in London, Paris, Frankfurt and New York. By this time, the Seligman family had grown to 104 persons, a very prolific group.

In 1867, Joseph terminated the San Francisco operation as unprofitable and gave the land to the city. He bought stock in the New York Mutual Gas Light Company, a predecessor of Consolidated Edison, the present monopoly, for pennies a share and soon made one million dollars on this transaction, as did Cornelius Vanderbilt. He could have purchased three square miles of Manhattan for $450 thousand, but passed this opportunity, which would have made his family the worlds richest, had he made the deal.

When Ulysses S. Grant became president, he wanted Joseph Seligman to be his Secretary of the Treasury. Joseph turned down this offer as also another one to run for Mayor of New York because of his business commitments.

During the late 1860s and 70s, the Seligmans dabbled in railroad stocks, financing dozens of railroads, but always losing money. By acting as an agent to Jay Gould of the Erie, he became involved unwittingly, in the gold scandal of this time.

In 1873, Joseph founded the Anglo California National Bank Ltd. Half a dozen years later he relinquished control of this San Francisco bank, which eventually became the Crocker Citizens' Bank.

Later, Joseph personally handled the affairs of President Lincoln's widow after she proved incapable of doing so. He even paid for Mrs. Lincoln and Todd Lincoln's move to Europe when she settled in Frankfurt, Germany. He helped to get Congress to award her a widow's pension. She later became insane.

Joseph hired Horatio Alger, the novelist, as tutor for his children. Joseph invested Horatio Alger's money from royalties for him and made Alger a rich man.

In 1874, the Seligman Banking House allied with the Rothschilds to sell American bonds in Europe and the United States. By 1880, the Seligmans were the undisputed leading banking house of America and were called "the American Rothschilds". Judge Henry Hilton (Hilton Hotel chain), of Boss Tweed's circle, became executor of the Grand Union Hotel in Saratoga, New York. After working for President Hayes in the Spring of 1877, to iron out a plan for refunding the balance of the Government war debt, Joseph decided to vacation at the Grand Union Hotel, where he had often stayed in the past. He was refused lodging because he was an "Israelite". This incident became nationally famous. Among the businesses that Judge Hilton ran was the A. T. Stewart store in Philadelphia. It was boycotted and thus failed and was sold to John Wanamaker. Joseph had not tried to be involved in such an issue as admittance of Jews to hotels, but his name made the issue a national one.

Joseph was involved in many Philanthropies, including the founding with Felix Adler of the Ethical Cultural Society, Jewish and Christian Charities and the helping of immigrants. His descendants are, to this day, involved in merchant banking but to a lesser degree. He was an advisor to five presidents and did yeoman service for his adopted country. Joseph Seligman died in 1879, while visiting his daughter in New Orleans.

Chapter VII

THE BARON DE HIRSCH FUND

Most people, including many of our own brethren do not visualize Jews as farmers. The history of farming by Jews in the United States, however, is replete with stories of pioneering, adventure, agricultural developments and the founding of the first agricultural university in the world. 1970 marks the 79th anniversary of the founding of the Baron De Hirsch Fund, the parent organization and forerunner of the Jewish Agricultural Society. Let us begin our story with the man who founded the fund and his part in Jewish farming in the entire world. Successive articles will deal with the achievements of the Jewish farmer in this country.

Maurice De Hirsch was born in 1831, the son of Baron Joseph De Hirsch, a wealthy court banker and landowner in Munich, Austria. By the age of twenty, Maurice had become able and experienced enough to join an international banking firm in Brussels. He later married the daughter of the bank president. In the years that followed, he displayed his financial genius world-wide, by building railroads in Turkey, Austria, the Balkans and Russia. He financed the development of sugar and copper companies. His growing fortune, plus his wife's inheritance, enabled him to underwrite huge enterprises worldwide.

Due to his early religious training and on seeing the plight of Jews in Eastern Europe during his business activities, Maurice resolved to help his fellow Jews. He figured that much of their plight was due to lack of skills and training. Keeping this in mind, in 1863, he donated a large sum of money to the Alliance Israelite to expand its system of primary and trade schools. He set up a foundation in Austria to provide vocational training. He helped many Jews to flee from Russia to Central and Western Europe and the USA. After his only son died, he retired and devoted his life to philanthropy.

Maurice offered the Czarist government fifty million francs to establish an educational system for Jews, but they refused. He knew that the Israelites of old were agriculturists par excellence, so he decided to reawaken this in his contemporary Jews.

A number of Jewish immigrants from Russia who had settled in South Jersey were in trouble and appealed to De Hirsch for help. So did many American Jewish leaders like Jesse Seligman, Jacob Schiff, Oscar Strauss and others. He gave help, and after lengthy negotiations, he started the Baron Be Hirsch fund in 1891, with $2,400,000 in the USA. In 1891, he also established a much larger organization in Europe called the Jewish Colonization Association (JCA), to which he ultimately gave a total of $36,000,000. He bought large tracts of land in Argentina and Brazil and settled 5,000 Jewish families in Argentina. This immigration was the foundation of the Jewish community in Argentina. The Baron died in 1896, but the fund he started continued. In 1900, a part of the fund became the Jewish Agricultural Society. The Fund also supported the Industrial Removal Office, which found jobs for Jewish immigrants in Cincinnati, Chicago, Louisville, and many other interior cities and paid their transportation costs there. The fund established a trade school in New York City, which was turned over to the City in 1935.

The fund started an agro-industrial colony in Woodbine, New Jersey and founded an agricultural school here. Countless other organizations were founded, financed or assisted by the fund. A half dozen other Jewish Agricultural colonies were established in the United States. The thousands of Jews the Baron helped to get to America were not matched by anyone else.

The Baron did not believe in alms giving or "charity". He believed in helping people to help themselves in order to become productive members of society. He wanted to establish Jewish farmers, handicraftsmen and tradesmen, in any land where Jews could exist as themselves with dignity and become responsible citizens.

Chapter VIII
THE JEWISH AGRICULTURAL SOCIETY

The Jewish Agricultural and Industrial Aid Society started in 1900 as a subsidiary of the Baron de Hirsch Fund. Its purpose was to promote the success of agricultural attempts by Jews. At first, the Society (JAS) financed small industries in farm regions to aid the Jewish farmer with another source of income. Both the industries' farms fared poorly because of competition from bigger firms and because the farms were too small to pay. Because of these failures, the industry was abandoned.

In the early 1900s, Jewish agricultural colonies were started in Tyler, Texas; Arpin, Wisconsin; Baltimore, Maryland; North Dakota; Farawide County, Wyoming; and Tary County, Washington. By 1915, all of these colonies had failed. The JAS concluded that the collective farm didn't fare too well in America. It then encouraged individual Jews who were interested in farming, and settled them near urban centers with goodly Jewish populations. In 1900, 300 families were aided; in 1909, 3,040 families in thirty-seven states were helped. Another 3,000 families were working farms without JAS help.

In 1908, the *Jewish Farmer*, an agricultural magazine in Yiddish, was first published. English was added later, and in the 1930s a German section was added for the influx of German Jewish farmers. Itinerant agricultural instructors were employed by the JAS. This was before the County Agency was started, mind you. In 1908, the Federation of Jewish Farmers of America was started which lasted until 1920. This started a number of successful cooperative feed mills. Fairs were held by the Jewish farm communities. These also started farm implement manufacturing, butter and egg processing, feed merchandising, etc. In New York

State alone, by 1912, there were about 1,500 families. The New York State College of Agriculture established an extension to work with Jewish farmers. These Jews started credit unions, followed by a fire insurance firm. In the Catskills, there were numerous Jewish farmers engaged in dairying, fruit and vegetables growing, egg production, boarding houses and hotel keeping.

In New Jersey, the JAS made hundreds of loans for starting chicken and egg farms. This set the pattern for the Federal agricultural credit – on easy terms – that soon started. The JAS consulted the group that started the Federal Land Banks. Mr. Robinson, manager of JAS, became the first president of the Springfield Federal Land Bank (for all of New England).

In 1924, the Immigration Act was passed, which reduced Jewish immigration dramatically. The Depression of the 1930s hurt many poultry farmers. Then, by-product industries started. Dr. Arthur Goldhaft, a noted veterinarian and son of an early Am Olam settler (older Jewish colonies), started the Vineland Poultry Laboratories. This lab became a purveyor of all kinds of vaccines in the entire United States and then overseas. Many poultry breeders and specialized broiler growers started their business. The cooperative egg auction was started. A special lab at the New Jersey College of Agriculture was started to perform research in poultry diseases. In New York, the Jews introduced cauliflower as a paying crop. The Potato king of Connecticut was a Jew.

By 1930, there were 80,000 Jews living on farms in the US. The JAS helped many of them save their farms during the Depression. The JAS settled hundreds of German Jewish refugees on farms prior to World War II. At the end of World War II, there were 20,000 Jewish families living on farms engaged in every branch of farming. The Jews excelled in research and scientific methods in farm operations. The JAS, together with the New York Association for New Americans, lent money to displaced persons from Hitler's Europe to start life anew on farms.

The JAS played a big part in helping to rehabilitate survivors of Nazism. In New Jersey, where many of them settled, the Jewish Poultry man's Association was organized in 1950. Thousands of refugees were settled between 1945–1954, all over the US by the JAS with its own funds.

A branch office of the JAS was opened in 1945, in Los Angeles because of the growth of Jewish farmers in Los Angeles and Petaluma. One of the big broiler game farmers is the Barlas Feed Mill in Petaluma.

In the last fifteen years, over half of the New England Jewish farmers have quit farming because of changing business conditions. There are now estimated to be 1,000 Jewish farmers in New Jersey, 2,000 in New York, 3,000 in California – about 7,000 in the United States.

Chapter IX

JEWISH FARMING IN CALIFORNIA AND THE PETALUMA STORY

In the past two chapters we have discussed the Baron de Hirsch Fund and the Jewish Agriculture Society (JAS) in the United States as well as farming by Jews in the United States. Closer to home, we will discuss a sketchy history of farming by Jews in California – sketchy because a complete account would fill several volumes. You may recognize some of the names and ranches, especially those of the B'nai B'rith Lodge in Petaluma. The Petaluma Lodge was a member of the Central California Council of B'nai B'rith Lodges, as was David Lubin in Sacramento, California.

The first Jewish settlers in California came from Germany and other Western European countries during the 1850s – the Gold Rush days. According to Jacob Maize, the manager of the Western office of the Jewish Agricultural Society (in Los Angeles) from 1945–1960, Jewish farmers and ranchers were prevalent in the 1860s. A famous traveler to California in 1859–61, I. J. Benjamin stated that in Los Angeles in 1860, the Jews had great flocks of sheep and herds of cattle. One hundred Jews lived there at that time. They also owned vineyards, the largest in the area belonging to a Mr. Morries. In San Bernardino, there were thirty Jews who engaged in agriculture, had ranches and big cattle herds.

The Israelite magazine, in 1864, stated that in Sonoma a large vineyard was operated by Louis Tichnor. In San Diego, many Jewish farmers existed, notably Joseph Menasse, Esq. The San Joaquin, Sonoma and San Jose Valleys and Contra Costa had a goodly number of Jewish farmers and ranchers.

In 1920, Sam Hamburg came to the US, worked his way through the Agricultural College in Davis, California, and soon leased 300 acres with the most modern equipment including crop dusting planes. He raised cotton, alfalfa, cantaloupes and sugar beets. He introduced cotton production in Israel and taught farm management practices used in large-scale farming in California.

Danny Dannenburg, of El Centro, shipped thousands of carloads of lettuce, cabbage, carrots and onions, with a payroll over one and a half million dollars. He started out on leased land in 1946 after he returned from the Army in World War II.

The David Freedman Company, of Thermal, California raised over fifteen crops. Mr. Lionel Steinberg, the manager, was a member of the White House Food for Peace Council. He has served on People-to-People Missions to many foreign countries including Russia and Israel. Colonel Irving Salomon of Escondido has a herd of 200 registered Hereford cattle and a number of Quarter horses, plus over 850 acres. There were over hundred notable Jewish ranchers and feeders in California.

Among large dairies were the Shein Brothers, Madera; William Strauss in Marin. The large farmers were Hyman Cheim, Marysville (peaches, pears, prunes, almonds, plums); Joe Helfand, Ontario (sweet potatoes, squash).

The story of Petaluma is a history in itself. It was the first organized Jewish rural community in California. Incidentally, the JAS did not have any part in its founding. In 1904, Sam Melnick from Lithuania settled there on seven acres. He built a small shack and started with 500 pullets, thus becoming the first Jewish poultry man in California. Later, he became the leading poultry man in the area with 16,000 chickens. His fame spread and Jewish families started to move there. By 1921, there were about sixty-five families there, most of whom had never been farmers. The older families of the area endorsed notes for the newer families and gave them advice. The Hebrew Free Loan Society of San Francisco helped with loans. In 1921, the price of eggs dropped from ninety-four cents per dozen to eighteen cents and almost bankrupted many of the families. The Abraham Haas Memorial Foundation established a $550,000 fund and saved many farmers. In 1925, a Jewish community center was built with the help of a $5,000 gift from Mrs. Abraham Haas.

In 1935, the ninety Jewish families became pioneers in the

broiler and fryer industry. During World War II, the Jewish farmers established a cooperative poultry-dressing plant. By the end of World War II, there were 175 Jewish farm families in Petaluma. A feed mill was established by the Barlas Brothers. Several other businesses in town were owned by Jews, but by and large, gentiles ran the businesses in town, while the Jews ran the farms.

In early 1950s, there were about 300 Jewish farm families in Petaluma, ten per cent of all the poultry farmers of Sonoma County. Today, there are about fifty Jewish poultry farms in Petaluma and trucks carrying poultry and eggs from Petaluma can be seen all over Northern California.

Julius Goldman of Egg City, Moorpark, California has over one and a half million layers. He has his own feed mill, a veterinarian, a laboratory, a poultry nutritionist and an experimental flock of 100,000 birds. He turns out 60,000 pounds of eggs per hour.

Mr. Jacob Maize of the JAS died in 1960 after performing yeoman service – helping hundreds of Jewish farmers, ranch hands, hired hands and others get started. The JAS is still there to help any of you who want to become farmers.

That's about all for now. I'm going into my backyard to pick some cucumbers for my wife to make kosher pickles, some tomatoes and acorn squash. I shall also "sit under my vine and fig tree (a small one), where none shall make me afraid" (a paraphrase from the book of Micah).

Chapter X
THE JEWS OF PARTHIA

You have all either read about or seen the motion picture where Spartacus led a slave army of reportedly 80,000 men across Rome in an effort to escape to freedom. Spartacus conquered everything in his path until the mighty General Crassus of Rome defeated his army. Crassus was well nigh invincible, until he met the Parthian army. His army was routed and almost annihilated, causing the start of the crack in the Roman Empire. And who led and formed a great part of the Parthians? Jews!

But we're getting ahead of our story. The ancient Hebrews came out of Ur in Mesopotamia. This was in Abraham's time, approximately 4,000 years ago. At that time, Ur was near to the sea. Even in Solomon's time the alluvial silt deposit that formed the coast of the Persian Gulf was about 100 miles north of where it is now. The Jews wandered all over this area, became traders in and with Babylon (Mesopotamia) both by land and by sea.

Later, when Cyrus of Persia conquered the Babylonians and permitted Jews to return to Jerusalem, the Persian Empire extended to Egypt. Cyrus and his Persian horsemen had conquered all the area of Persia, Babylonia, Assyria and a dozen lesser countries. An era of Jewish peace under Persian rule began.

There were Jewish communities in 127 provinces of the Persian Empire according to the Book of Esther. Jews were respected, educated, wealthy and had some measure of power. They were educators, road builders, engineers and merchants on an international scale (of the known world). Susa was the capital of Persia and had a large Jewish population.

Out of the Northern highlands of Persia roared the Parthians, fierce, wild, untamed, master horsemen. They overthrew Greek rule in the 3rd century B.C.E. in much of the Old Persian Empire. The Parthians and Jews both were, or had been, nomads and there developed a great affinity between the two peoples. The Parthians had great respect for the code by which the Jews conducted themselves. Thousands of Parthians became Jewish. Their war chiefs and thousands of their common people also became Jewish. This fact became well known to the Romans who tried to extend their empire into Persia. For 300 years, legions of Romans could not defeat the Parthians. In fact, many of these legions were wiped out of existence.

The union of Parthia with Jewish life flourished to its maximum in Babylonia. Here the Babylonian Talmud was put together in its finished form. Overland routes were opened to China and India as well as sea routes by Jewish ships and merchants. Jewish synagogues were built all over Persia.

The Persians finally regained their power and defeated the Parthian cavalry. Since the Jews were so closely a part of the Parthians, they too suffered. Added to the fact that so many Parthians were Jewish was the fact that the Persians had embraced the Zoroastrian religion. Zoroastrianism had monotheistic elements but was dualistic. Although highly ethical in beliefs, Zoroastrianism could not be accepted by Jews because of its dualism.

Dualism sees the universe and the world as a dueling ground for the forces of good and Evil, God against Satan, light against darkness, etc. The Jews believed that God was the Creator of all elements and forces – peace, light, darkness, evil – and could, therefore, not accept Zoroastrianism.

The "Z's" saw enough similarities between Judaism and "Z", that they thought Judaism was a mockery of "Z". So until the Arab Moslems overthrew the Persians in 642 C.E. the Jews were persecuted severely at times and were driven into hiding or silence.

Chapter XI
THE JEWS AND THE VIKINGS

Most of us think, based on what we have been exposed to, that the Viking only stormed out of his retreat, hacked off heads, raped and stole women, plundered, burned and returned to his home base. This is not quite true. As with all peoples who are seafaring and come into contact with other cultures, they became traders and merchants.

The Viking was a highly civilized and worldly man at that time. Much like the Jew, he was a wandering trader, who would do business wherever his long ships would carry him. He took his long ships into the Atlantic and Mediterranean, not simply to loot and burn, but to engage in commerce.

Legend has it that even while Jesus lived, Jews were building log synagogues in the German forests and stone synagogues on the Baltic shores. There is evidence that the Jews had trade relations with the Prussians as far back as the 3rd century C.E. Now what do the Vikings have to do with the Prussians? Or the Jews for that matter? The Prussians were neither Germans nor Christians. They were a Slavic group with strong Viking influence and much intermarriage. In fact, Kiev in the Ukraine was built along the Dnieper River by the Vikings who controlled the area. The Jews lived and traded peacefully with the pagan Prussians.

In the 5th century C.E., someone in India learned to weave pure gold as thread. It was then woven into Indian cotton. This material brought three or four times the price of silk in the fifth, sixth and seventh centuries. You could get twenty pounds of gold for one pound of this cloth. To the Vikings, this cloth meant status of the highest order. The Vikings had looted Gaelic and Roman towns and had all the gold, silver and pottery they could ever use. When the Jewish trader spread out a cotton scarf woven with gold, this miracle was worth any price.

Also, there was no Viking who had not heard of the Tyrian purple, the "cloth of the gods", or "Jew cloth", as it was commonly called. This was silk made by Jews who had raised silkworms in Sicily, southern Italy and Greece and had then dyed the silk purple, the color of royalty. The Vikings controlled the ambergris trade at that time. The ambergris comes from the whale and is used to make the essence of perfumes. It is very expensive, needless to say. The Jew traded his cloth, perfume and silk, for ambergris and gold.

In the eighth, ninth and tenth centuries, Jewish trading posts existed along the Baltic shores. Trade with the Viking long ships was brisk and profitable. The Jews brought Chazarian furs, silk, linen, cotton, royal purple cloth, jewels, perfumes, spices and medicines. The Jews also functioned as surgeons, physicians, and pharmacists, for the Jewish practice of medicine was highly organized as far back as the time of Christ and Hillel. Many wounded or ailing Vikings were treated by Jewish physicians.

In the 12th century, the Order of the Teutonic Knights (German Crusaders) moved against the Prussians (who, as previously indicated, were pagans) and started exterminating them, the Jews among them. Eventually, most of the original Prussians were wiped out. The Prussians of the last 400 years are mostly descendants of the Germanic Knights and Germans who followed them. These Crusaders also destroyed all of the Jewish trading posts on the Baltic shores.

The Jews had rapport with the Vikings and always fared reasonably well with them. When the Vikings conquered the coast of France and soon became Normans, they treated the Jews as equals. When the Vikings conquered Sicily, the Jews fared well; in fact, by the 15th century, there were 100,000 Jews in Sicily. When the Norman of Viking origin conquered England, he took Jews into England with him. The Jews, consequently, were disliked by the Saxons.

The Vikings brought their maps and shoreline charts of the Mediterranean from the Jewish cartographers in Majorca. It is also believed that because of their close contact, the Jews had such good maps of the Atlantic coast of Europe.

The present day Swedes are descendants of the Vikings. The

Jewish presence in Sweden dates back 1000 years in a commercial sense, rather than a communal sense. Jews who went to Sweden became Swedes. By the year 1956, there were only 13,000 Swedes who identified themselves as Jews. Intermarriage between the Jews and Swedes and the Jews and the Danes began with the Viking period. Maybe there is a lesson here for those who want to see Judaism fade out of the picture – treat them well, as equals, as partners and eventually, they become part of you, not a group apart.

Chapter XII
ARABIA – REFUGE OF THE JEWS

Arabia is the world's largest peninsula (half a million square miles) connected to Egypt, through Israel, and to Turkey, through Syria. The Bedouin and Quraish Arabs have lived here since the beginning of recorded history. The religion of the peoples was of the nature-worship type – heaven, stars, trees, stones, etc. Eventually, this blended into the worship of a black meteorite, the Black Stone, which is the Kaaba (cube) in Mecca. The Bedouins lived in the desert, while the Quraish lived along the coastal areas where they established trading villages and dealt with the Bedouins for the booty they robbed from caravans. This was the extent of commerce until the Jews began to arrive in the end of the 1ˢᵗ century C.E. Commerce and industry began to expand, cities grew and art became important. The Jews came to Arabia, because in 70 C.E. the Romans had taken Jerusalem and made life bitter for the Jews in that area.

The immigration of Jews started as a trickle but by the fifth and sixth centuries, it became a flood. The reason for this was the power struggle between the Sassanid and Byzantine empires, causing Jews to leave Syria and Palestine. These two warring empires made a truce between themselves and started slaughtering Jews, Lebanese, Syrians and others who happened to be in their path.

The Jews introduced handicrafts, goldsmithing and the date palm. The date palm became to the Arabs what the potato became to the Irish. The Jews founded Medina and helped the Quraish Arabs raise their villages into cities. They made Mecca the San Francisco of the Middle East. When Christian armies came to proselytize and plunder, the Jews joined the Arabs in defeating them, for the Jews were grateful to the Arabs for giving them a home. Many pagan Arabs were attracted to Judaism because of its monotheism, devotion to family, life and education for its young. The Jews were called the "People of the Book". In peace, both lived side by side, respecting and dealing with each other.

The Old Testament was studied and discussed by the Arabs. The ideology and monotheism of the Jews was blended, without contradiction, with their nature-worship by many Arabs. The Jews lived in Arabia 500 years before Mohammed was born (569–632 C.E.).

Mohammed was orphaned at six years of age and brought up with no education. At twelve years of age, he was taken to Syria by caravan and came into contact with both Judaism and Christianity. The Jewish patriarchs became his heroes. At twenty-five, he married a rich widow and was still illiterate. At the age of forty, Mohammed believed that he had a revelation, which made him the successor to Moses and Jesus. He converted his family, relatives and his slaves. He tried to do the same with the Quraish Arabs, but to them he was a dangerous radical, and he was forced to flee from Mecca. He went to Medina, hoping to convince the Jews (of whom he thought very highly) to support him. Why not? His own religion was based on Judaism and, therefore, the Jews should join him. But, like with all Messiahs before him, the Jews rejected him. He then decided to turn against the Jews, for the wrath of a rejected suitor is bitter. He decided that the Quraish armies wouldn't stop him if he used his small army to conquer the Jews of Medina, if they thought he was going to share the wealth of the Jews. So he made war on the Jews, took their wealth but "double-crossed" the Quraish who had sat by waiting for their share of the booty. Mohammed used this wealth to equip an army of 10,000 men and marched against Mecca. Too late, the Quraish realized they had made a big mistake in not aligning themselves with the Jews. Seeing the big army of Mohammed they surrendered. Within two years, all of Arabia was under Mohammed's rule. He called his religion Islam, and it became the religion of Arabia. He died in 632 C.E. and the mantle of succession fell to Abu-Bekr. The hostility towards the Jews, which Mohammed had manufactured out of political expediency, vanished soon after his death.

Chapter XIII

THE JEWS IN MUFTI

You have read of the place where the Jews had found a haven in Arabia, that vast peninsula of desert with an oasis of modern civilization – civilization due in great part to the influx of Jews and the Arabs dealing with them as almost equals.

After the death of Mohammed and the rule of Abu-Bekr, the Jews once again experienced freedom to grow. Prior to this, they had fought the influence of Grecian culture, detested the Epicureans, disavowed the Greek philosophers. Now the Jews expanded their horizons, for none tried to "ghettoize" them. They became astronomers, alchemists, doctors, finance ministers, architects and mathematicians. They accepted the best of Hellenism and Arabism and expanded and enlarged their horizons.

They opened international business offices in Cairo, Bagdad, Cordoba. The Arabs wanted to have the Greek literary and scientific works to increase their status and scientific knowledge. They wished to have the Greek translated into Arabic. Whom could the Arabs ask to perform this task but the Jews, for the Jews of the Arabian Empire spoke Hebrew, Arabic, Latin, Greek, Persian and Syriac? Jews started in about 750 C.E. to work on this task: first translating the Syriac and Greek into Arabic, then into Hebrew. They then used their influence on the Arabs by translating Hebrew literature and philosophy into Arabic. By the 12th century, the works of the Jewish scholars had spread through Europe. King Frederick II (King of the Romans, the Germans and King of Jerusalem) appointed Jewish scholars to teach Hebrew in Naples. He wanted Hebrew works to be translated into Latin.

One of the scholars was Ibn Daud. He translated Hebrew, Greek and Arabic into Latin. He introduced Arabic numerals into European math. He also brought the concept of the "zero" into math. Euclid and the Babylonian Talmud were translated into Latin by other Jewish scholars, as well as Plato and Sophocles.

You must understand that Greek culture was so pervasive, so thought provoking with logic and reason intertwined, that even to this day, it is one of the world's great influences. The Jews of that period fought hard to stay Jews, but they almost became Greeks because of their outstanding logic. Even then, the Jews encircled their faith with Greek thought, logic, and philosophy, and proved stronger than Greek thought without faith. The Jews, according to some historians, are the inheritors and carriers of the Greek cultural tradition.

The Jews then broadened their language and writings into secular matters and brought out a dictionary. Even then, Jewish poets were expounding on the miracle of Jewish survival. Can you imagine that – over 600 years ago! The Arab sultans and rulers welcomed Jewish doctors, philosophers, and scientists. They became personal aides of many Arabic emperors.

But time marches on. Wild tribesmen became raiding armies, then nations, and the advent of one such group under Genghis Khan overran the Islamic Empire, slaughtering hundreds of thousands of people. With the Christians, Sassanids and Mongols, the Islamic Empire gradually broke apart into small pieces. While it lasted, which was almost as long as the Roman Empire, the Jews, for the most part, prospered and contributed to the advancement of mankind.

Chapter XIV
VLADIMIR JABOTINSKY (1880–1940)

One of the most colorful figures in recent Jewish history is Zev Jabotinsky. If there ever was a real Jewish Defense League, Zev could be credited with founding it, as he did on a number of occasions. He was born in Russia, under the Czarist regimes, where the Jew lived in perpetual persecution. Zev was a very learned man. By the time he was eighteen, he served as a foreign correspondent for Odessa newspapers in Rome, writing under the pen name of Altalena for three years. Aware of the plight of the Jews upon his arrival back in Russia, he started organizing Jewish self-defense units. He argued for the Jews' minority rights. He also fought for the revival of Hebrew. His articles were read by many people, for he wrote in Russian, Hebrew and later, in English.

In World War I, he advocated recruiting Jewish regiments to fight on the Palestine front. From his efforts, the Zion Mule Corporation was established in 1915. In 1917, under British command, Jabotinsky served in one of these regiments. He organized the first Jewish defense league (Haganah) in Jerusalem and led it during the bloody Arab onslaught in 1920. For this, the British sentenced him to fifteen years in prison, but he only served about six months.

Zev was always opposing Zionist groups for being too timid and not taking a forceful enough stand. In 1925, he formed the World Union of Revisionists; because he considered the official Zionists a bunch of "do nothings". In 1929, he began to advocate secession from the combined Zionist groups (Jewish Agency), because they refused to say that their aim was to establish a Jewish state. So he formed the New Zionist Organization and urged the rapid aliyah (immigration) of Eastern European Jews to Palestine.

In 1936, the Grand Mufti, with arms supplied by the Nazis,

started attacking cities and villages all over Palestine. Jabotinsky wanted to counter-attack with the Haganah, but their official policy was only defense. He violently disagreed with this policy and wanted to counter-attack both the British and Arabs. So he organized an underground paramilitary force (the Irgun) to fight the Arabs, for the British to leave Palestine and to declare Palestine's independence. Many young Jews joined the Irgun and fought both British and Arabs.

When World War II broke out, Zev again demanded a Jewish army. A number of Jewish volunteers fought at Tobruk in Northern Africa. 130,000 Jews joined the British Africa Corps, but the British only accepted 30,000 because they didn't trust them. Jabotinsky was a real fighter, a man of action, yet a scholar. He translated Dante and Poe into Hebrew, wrote an auto-biography in English, and translated Bialik's poetry into Russian. He also wrote Russian poetry along with Russian novels. When you go to Israel, be sure to see the statue built in his honor. He was quite a man!

Chapter XV
THE ORIGIN OF YIDDISH

Yiddish is a language with Jewish or Semitic roots. Jews who followed the Roman legions in their conquests as traders, merchants, storekeepers, etc., moved from France and Italy into the heartland of Germany. The Germanic tribes spoke coarse, semi-barbaric Teutonic dialects. By the 3rd century C.E., most of the soldiers were German. In the Frankish-Gothic-Germanic heartland of Europe, the trading dialect had to have a Teutonic base, and that broad base congealed into some sort of order in the Rhineland.

By the 7th century, in and around the city of Cologne, the largest Jewish community in Germany had come into being as the heart of commerce and trading at that time. In this area, the Jewish language of Yiddish came into being. It spread and moved wherever Jews moved to do business. At this time, Germanic lettering in the Gothic script was very much varied and primitive, and frequently unreadable. To simplify matters for themselves, the Jews wrote this language in the Hebrew script, which they had been using for over 2,000 years. The base of the language was Germanic, but the dialects were in the speech of semi-barbaric tribesmen. The speech was limited to familiar objects and uncomplicated actions, weapons and mundane objects. No philosophical, esoteric, or creative thought, or even discussion was possible. Jewish life and memory encompassed the history and philosophy of many lands and the Germanic language was inadequate for expressing philosophy of many lands. So the Jews added French and Roman (Italian) words for their sophisticated adjectives and artistic expression. There was still an enormous void, so the Jews borrowed Hebrew words for philosophical, geographical, social and religious content. So far, we have mostly Teutonic, a smattering of French and Italian and a fair amount of

Hebrew. A few Russian and Polish words were also added. Since every Jewish child could read Hebrew, he soon learned Yiddish and could speak it, somewhat akin to Pidgin English. It, therefore, became part of the Jews. In fact, the word "Ashkenazi", which the Northern and Central European Jews are called, means "German", in the Hebrew language.

The horrible Crusaders came along with the relentless passage of time, and hundreds of thousands of Jews were slaughtered, driven out, or enslaved. In Germany, the Crusaders and peasants alike, treated the Jews worst of all. Some bishops tried to protect the Jews of their own towns, but by and large, were unsuccessful. In Cologne, the townspeople took the Jews into their homes and told the Crusaders to pass by or take the city with fire and sword. The Crusaders held off until they learned that Archbishop Hermann, of Cologne, decided the Jews would be safer distributed among seven neighboring villages. They waited for this to happen, then killed every last man, woman, and child in each place.

When the Jews left Germany, they took their Yiddish with them. They went to Poland and Lithuania where the heathens (then) treated them more kindly. The reason for this is that Christianity had not taken hold yet in these places.

By the fourteenth and fifteenth centuries, the language had changed very little. The German language became modern and aggressive and formal, while Yiddish stayed informal, more familiar forms being used. Yiddish softened, became gentle and more slurred. By this time, Jews were all over Europe. Yiddish literature developed in the Ghettos, which came into being after the Crusades. All the great classics of the world were translated into Yiddish. Theaters, newspapers, schools, poems and philosophical works developed. About 12,000,000 people were then speaking Yiddish.

When the Jews were driven out of one country, they took Yiddish to another. For specific examples, from Poland into France, from Lithuania into England, from Russia into the United States, and then to Latin America. As the Jews became more accepted into the life of Germany, the Jews there spoke German, not Yiddish. The Jews who left Germany and Europe took Yiddish with them.

Yiddish is about 1,300 years old, and may only last about a hundred more years. Hebrew will probably replace it, as it has been used continuously by Jews for over 3,300 years. For many of us, the Yiddish language of our parents and grandparents brings a warm feeling of contentment, of nostalgia, of appreciation. After all, in what other language can a word describe so much with so much feeling? As a matter of fact, the National Yiddish Book Center (NYBC) of Amherst, Mass, under the guidance of Aaron Lansky, is doing a yeoman job of reviving the use of Yiddish. The NYBC has raised about six million dollars to build the center. Folks will be trained in Yiddish. Books have been requested by countries worldwide. They could still use donations to carry on their work. Also the "Forward" newspaper is now published weekly in English, Yiddish and Russian.

Chapter XVI
DR. IMMANUEL VELIKOVSKY

One of the most controversial scientists of this century is dead. He passed away at his home in Princeton, New Jersey, November 17, 1979 at the age of eighty-four. He had been in weakening health for several years, his indomitable spirit prosaically conquered at last, by diabetes.

Velikovsky emerged into worldwide prominence in 1950, with the publication of his most famous book, *Worlds in Collision*, which described the near encounters of the Earth with Venus and Mars in ancient, though historical times, making him the focus of a scientific conflict for thirty years.

This book was followed by the first of his historical series, *Ages in Chaos* (1952), which he called his magnum opus, attempting a massive reconstruction of what he considered a confused chronology of ancient Egyptian history, from the middle of the second millennium B.C. down to the post Alexandrian time of Ptolemy II.

Velikovsky's approach to geology and paleontology, as exemplified in *Earth in Upheaval* (1955), might best be described as secular catastrophism, since he was opposed to fundamentalism. He accepted the basic tenets of evolutionary theory, but with the provision that cataclysmic events caused discontinuities in the record of stones and bones, bringing whole genera to extinction and causing wholesale mutations in surviving species, while mountains were overturned and the land and sea exchanged places.

Such interdisciplinary researches, which necessitated broad excursions into dozens of scientific and historic fields, attracted a few assenting scholars at first, while alienating most of the academic community. Since Velikovsky's work ran counter to more than a century of developed thought, he was initially considered to be just another voice in the wilderness who had little grasp of the problems and issues.

His "advance claims" of the high thermal history of the planet Venus, the wandering geographic pole of Earth, the lunar-like desolation of Mars, the radio noises of Jupiter, the chlorine-shroud of Saturn and some seventy-odd other predictions, all based on his historical researches – earned for Velikovsky increasing scorn and vituperation. But he never returned these "compliments" in kind.

As many of these claims were confirmed – and there still are quite a few to be investigated – they were classed as lucky guesses, because the hard sciences did not recognize the sociological framework from which these predictions came. Velikovsky demanded too much in the way of revolutionary changes to be taken seriously.

Velikovsky himself was a product of revolutionary times. He was born on June 10, 1895, in Nitebsk, Russia, of Jewish parentage, during an era of renaissance in scientific and sociological thought. During his youth, he formally studied mathematics at the Medvednikov Gymnasium in Moscow, and became proficient in six languages, graduating with honors.

He began premedical studies in the natural sciences at Montpelier, France, and continued at the University of Edinburgh, Scotland, after a side trip to Palestine (1914). During World War I, he studied law and ancient history at Moscow's Free University, and later received his medical degree from the University of Moscow.

Velikovsky spent two-plus years in exile with his parents, in the Ukraine and Caucasus after his father's land speculation in Palestine attracted the attention of the new Communist regime.

Velikovsky spent the next few years in Berlin, editing and preparing the two-volume, multilingual *Scripta Universitatis* with Heinrich Loewe, librarian at the University of Berlin. This work was conceived as the cornerstone of the Hebrew University in Jerusalem, the edifice of an idea, which had lain dormant since 1897. Velikovsky enlisted the aid of Albert Einstein and other world-renowned scholars. It was completed as ground-breaking began on the Hebrew University in 1924, being formally presented at the inauguration, a year later.

In 1923, Velikovsky married Elisheva Kramer, a violin student under Adolph Busch, and later a noted sculptress in her own right. After completion of the *Scripta Universitatis*, they moved to Palestine where Velikovsky practiced medicine for several years. He then undertook psychiatric training from Wilhelm Strekel, a student of Sigmund Freud, and began the practice of psycho-analysis.

Over the years, Velikovsky published a number of papers on psychology, a few in Freud's own *Imago*. In 1931, he wrote a now famous paper suggesting that pathological encephalograms would be found characteristic of epilepsy, which has since become a standard diagnostic technique. By 1939, he had outlined a monograph on Freud's *Moses and Monotheism* and came to the United States to complete his research. This outline eventually became his *Oedipus and Akhenaton* (1960), but his researches into ancient myths at the time suggested that vast natural catastrophes had decimated the Earth on numerous occasions.

Further work seemed to confirm Velikovsky's early suspicions, and continuing studies, abetted by the Second World War, led to his residing in the United States for the rest of his life. In 1942, he had completed an early draft of the historical *Ages in Chaos*. Robert Pfeiffer, chairman of Harvard's Department of Semitic Languages reviewed the manuscript favorably, but it wasn't to be published for another ten years.

In the meantime, Velikovsky worked on *Worlds in Collision*, so that by 1946 it was ready to be reviewed by critical scientists who – it was hoped – could affirm or deny that the planet Venus was still extremely hot, giving credence to ancient claims of rains of naphtha; and that it had an anomalous rotation, giving substance to the idea of massive perturbations during the close encounters.

No one in the scientific community could or would pick up the challenge. Nevertheless, only one publisher, Macmillan, saw any potential in the book, and in 1947, signed a tentative contract.

Within three years, Macmillan turned its rights to this bestseller over to Doubleday, while Velikovsky, undaunted, prepared the subsequent historical and scientific arguments. And the ensuing years saw only a gradual diminution of the outburst, which greeted *Worlds in Collision*.

Between 1960 and 1972, Velikovsky went into a semi-retirement to further develop his historical works, emerging when renewed interest in his ideas spread to the National Aeronautics and Space Administration, where Velikovsky lectured at colloquia, in 1972 at NASA Ames Research Center in California, and again in 1973 at NASA Langley, in Virginia. And this was in addition to a number of other academic and industrial sponsored lectures and presentations, including an honorary doctorate from the University of Lethbridge, Alta, in 1974.

A comprehensive answer to Velikovsky's critics, *The Age of Velikovsky*, came out in 1976. And, the scholar's continuation of his historical series recommenced with *Peoples of the Sea* (1977), followed by *Ramses II and Time* (1978), the *Dark Ages of Greece*, and the *Assyrian Conquest*, now in press. However, his planned swan song, *Mankind in Amnesia*, returning once again to his training forte, psychoanalyzing the motivations of the entire human race, still lies in manuscript form.

Velikovsky's personal quest has now ended, quietly and peacefully. All the arguments against him have been used up, save one, and this one may have been the most powerful of all: An objective discussion of his thesis. But since it was not, this initiative is lost.

The knee-jerk reaction to Velikovsky's work was not, after all, an aberration as such, but an integral process by which innovative creations are eventually accepted. It is believed that his work will be accepted as additions to knowledge of history, scientific endeavors and geology.

Chapter XVII

THEODOR (BENJAMIN ZEV) HERZL

Very few men have had such a profound effect on the course of Jewish history in the last hundred years as had Theodor Herzl. He is credited with being the founder of political Zionism, the embryo that led to the birth of the State of Israel. It is difficult to condense all that has been written into a few words, therefore, of necessity only documented historical occurrences will be mentioned.

Herzl was born in Budapest, Hungary, in 1860 of a rather well-to-do family. He studied in Vienna from 1878 to 1884 and became a freelance writer. He was pretty much of a playboy, and a ladies-man and caused some embarrassment to his father by his affairs d'amour. He achieved success as a social dramatist. In 1891, the paper, *The Viennese New Free Press*, sent him to Paris as their correspondent. Up until this time, he was not much interested in Jewish affairs or in the plight of European Jewry. But his experiences in Paris made him very much aware of the fact that he was a Jew, and he began to write articles concerning the Jews and their poor treatment.

For a while Herzl believed that by assimilating, the Jewish problems would end, but by 1894 he had changed his mind. He wrote a drama, *The New Ghetto* that caused much discussion. That same year, when the Dreyfus trial broke, he became deeply involved, not only because he was the correspondent of a newspaper, but because he saw a man being railroaded as a convenient scapegoat because he was a Jew, and therefore, more acceptable to the masses as a "traitor" than if he were a Christian. He wrote to many famous and notable Jews for their support to aid Captain Dreyfus. Not even the writings of another famous Frenchman, Emile Zola, helped at that time.

Herzl then decided that the Jews should have a state of their own. Baron de Hirsch, who founded the start of the Jewish Agricultural Society and many other Jewish charities, did not believe Herzl's ideas to be practical. In 1896, Herzl wrote and had published *Der Judenstadt* – The Jewish State. He stated that immigration was impractical and that by so doing, the Jews would be brought down to an economic and social level of the poorest peasants; that a Jewish state founded by international agreement was the solution; that the Jews should choose a territory of their own desires, but that logically, it should be Palestine. The assimilationists and ultra-Orthodox (Jews) both opposed this upstart who dared to write thus, but the youth and others rallied to his side. In 1896, he returned to Vienna as the literary editor of his paper, but devoted most of his time to Zionism.

Literally, from "scratch" with no money of any size, with no backing from Jewish financiers, Herzl moved mountains. He established contacts with the Duke of Baden, and with the Turkish Grand Vizier, whom he offered financial assistance in return for an independent Jewish state. Turkey, at that time (and for 400 years), had ruled Palestine. He single-handedly negotiated with rulers, statesmen, financiers who ruled Europe – the Kaiser, the Sultan of Turkey, Joseph Chamberlain, and Lord Lansdowne in England, Ministers Plehve and Witte in Russia, the Pope, Cardinal Merry del Val, the king of Italy, Baron de Hirsch, the Rothschilds and many others.

In 1897, Herzl had convened the First Zionist Congress at Basle, Switzerland, to unite various Jewish factions. Because of his success at obtaining interviews with nobility and heads of government and his successful writing, most groups attended. Herzl was elected President. He, of course, was criticized by many Jewish leaders and accused of having delusions of grandeur. Indeed, Herzl did become possessed of a dream, a Jewish state, and would not rest until it was culminated.

In 1899, the Jewish Colonial Trust was founded to aid in colonization of such a state. Kaiser Wilhelm II expressed his sympathy for this cause. Sultan Abdul Hamid of Turkey offered Herzl land outside of Palestine, including Wadi el Arish in the Sinai Peninsula. At various times, the British were considering offering Cyprus to the Jews and then Uganda. At the sixth Zionist

Congress, so much argument ensued over the offer of Uganda to the Jews, that Herzl had practically worked himself to death traveling, negotiating, meeting rejection after rejection, being criticized by his own people. He died at Edlach, Austria in 1904, of a heart condition, and was buried in Austria. Later, his remains were reburied on Mt. Herzl, near Jerusalem in 1949.

Marvin Lowenthal, in 1962, published the complete *Diaries of Theodor Herzl*. The interviews, emotions and hopes, of Herzl and the Who's Who of famous rulers and personages are captivating. It shows that a man with a dream can change the world. Maybe not in his own lifetime, but in those of his children or grandchildren.

We are all here but a short time on this Earth, but without our little contributions to Jewish survival, there would be no survival. We Jews have been priests unto the world, as it says in the Torah, for we have contributed much to man's progress in many fields, to advance the knowledge and well-being of mankind. Someday, by our efforts, Jerusalem and Israel will be the center for world peace and law, and "all nations will flow unto it". Be a part of it all, and move the dream further to reality!

Chapter XVIII

HEROD THE GREAT (A NON-HERO)

Gnaeus Pompey led the military campaign in the Third Mithridatic War (74–64 B.C.E.). These three Mithridatic wars brought the empire that Alexander had created into the Roman orbit. During that third Mithridatic War, however, Judah was overcome and made a vassal state of Rome. Pompey was one of the Roman generals with ambitions of great power. From his many victories, he took much plunder and returned to Rome resolved to be number one in the Roman Empire. But two other Roman generals had the same idea – Marcus Crassus and Julius Caesar. Neither of the three could get the upper hand, so they decided to compromise. They merged into what became the First Triumvirate. Since these three all had great ambitions, another war in 48 B.C.E. resulted in the death of this merger. Pompey was defeated and fled to Egypt.

When Pompey had conquered Judah, he started the wheels of fortune on a relentless downward path for the Jews. He appointed an Idumean to be his governor, which leads us to the point of this story.

Hyrcanus, the high priest, became the ethnarch (ruler), for he didn't put up any obstacles in Pompey's way to a peaceful rule. Pompey also named Antipater as political adviser to Hyrcanus. Aristobolus and Hyrcanus (brothers) were descended from the Hasmoneans (of Maccabean fame). Antipater, however, was an Idumean. He proceeded to do all he could to gain power. One of his first steps was to defeat Aristobolus (the former king) by aiding Hyrcanus.

One of the early Maccabean rulers, John Hyrcanus, had forcibly converted the Idumeans to Judaism around 115 B.C.E. Idumea was one of Judah's provinces and, for the help which Antipater gave the present Hyrcanus, Antipater was made governor of Idumea.

When Pompey was defeated in 48 B.C.E., Caesar took over Judah (now renamed Judea). Antipater played up to Caesar and was named administrator of Judea. After Caesar was assassinated, Antipater still played politics with one of his assassins, the very influential Cassius. So he stayed in power until his own family poisoned him in 43 B.C.E. Antipater's son Herod succeeded him.

Like father, like son. Herod then played up to Augustus, who became the new Caesar. Augustus then made Herod the king of the Jews. Herod, an Idumean, now ruled the Idumeans, who had previously converted to Judaism. And now we see the old adage come true – "The sins of the fathers are visited on the sons". What happens next reads like a horror story.

Herod then had Hyrcanus executed. His brother Aristobolus was captured by the Romans, sent to Rome and was poisoned. The last remaining brother, Antigonus, escaped to Parthia where he mustered an army and marched against Jerusalem. The Parthians were very friendly to the Jews and had previously converted in large numbers to Judaism of their own free will. They looked upon Jerusalem as their spiritual center. The Parthians were fierce warriors and they succeeded in driving out the Romans from recapturing Judea, but the Romans sent so many reinforcements that they finally recaptured Jerusalem in 37 B.C.E.

Herod now executed Antigonus, the last remaining Hasmonean male descendant. He also executed most of the Sanhedrin – forty-five members to be exact – as conspirators. He murdered anyone who he considered a threat to him. He murdered his favorite wife and three of his sons. He ordered – in one edict – all male infants to be executed in Bethlehem (according to the New Testament).

But to placate the Jews somewhat, he married a Hasmonean princess, Marianne (one of ten wives) and had two sons through this union. He went to murder these two sons also. Herod was a real madman, but he also was a great builder. He rebuilt the Temple of Solomon, palaces, roads and fortresses all over the place. One of these was Masada. He was succeeded (on his death) by two of his sons from a Samaritan wife, but one of these,

Archelaus was as bad, if not worse, than Herod. The Jews petitioned Augustus Caesar to depose him and their wish was granted. No more Jewish kings now, just Roman procurators. These procurators in the main, were money-hungry leeches who tried to squeeze every shekel they could out of the Jews until the Jews revolted in 66 C.E. In 70 C.E., the Romans destroyed Jerusalem and the temple, which Herod had rebuilt.

So that's the moral of this true story – never impose an idea or belief on someone by force – only by reason, example and tolerance. A few bad grapes can spoil a whole vat full of vintage wine.

Chapter XIX

THE FATE OF THE LOST TEN TRIBES OF ISRAEL

Mr. I. J. Benjamin, the worldwide traveler, really gave specifics about the sites of the tombs of many prophets and Israeli heroes like Daniel, Ezra, Joshua, and others. He also quoted the Bible and evidences of his investigation as to what happened to the various tribes. He spent a year in India and saw much evidence of Jewish settlement. Here is his account:

> In the reign of Menahem ben Gadi, Pul, the king of Assyria, invaded the Holy Land, but was paid a "war tax" of 1000 "centners" of silver to withdraw. (II Kings 15:19) In I Chronicles 5:26, Assyrian Kings Pul and Tiglath – pilneser carried away the tribes of Reuben, Gad and half the tribe of Manasseh and took them to Halah Habor and Hara, and to the shores of the river Ganges (all in India).

> At a different time, Tiglath – pilneser carried away the tribe of Naphtali into Assyria. (II Kings 15:29 and Isaiah 1:11) In the ninth year of Hoshea ben Elah, Shalmaneser, King of Assyria, again invaded. After a three-year-siege of Samaria, he carried away the rest of the ten tribes to Assyria. (II Kings 17:6) The Jews were then dispersed to Egypt, Ethiopia and Persia. King Cyrus, of Persia, permitted the Jews to return to the Holy Land, especially the tribes of Judah and Benjamin.

The "Islands of the West" are also mentioned which refer to the West Indies. India and China (Sinim) and Nubia, in Africa, are also mentioned.

In 1849, Mr. Benjamin spoke of Jewish families of Sassoon, Ezra, and David, in India. More will be written on the Jews and Tartars, Jewish bandit tribes of the Arabian Desert and the Jews of

China.

I. J. Benjamin traveled for eight years in Asia and Africa. He also went to the Philippines and China and later even visited the United States. He was very moved when he first arrived in Jerusalem. He recounts its history as follows:

> Shem, the son of Noah, began to build the walls of the city. Its earliest name was Salem, but after the proposed sacrifice of Isaac by Abraham, Abraham called the place Yirre. From this came the name Yerusalem. Twenty-five years after the liberation of the Israelites from Egypt, the city was governed by Jubusse, the successor of Abimelech. Jubusse completed the walls of the city and erected a fortress, which he called Jebus. When King David came to power, he came with an army against Jerusalem and the Jebusites and captured it. His son, Solomon, started the temple, which took seven years to build (480 years after the exodus from Egypt).

> The temple was destroyed, the Jews disbursed, the temple was rebuilt and destroyed again, and the Jews again were dispersed. Several monarchs and one caliph tried to rebuild the temple and failed. There were six gates to the city, five open and one always closed. After the Roman Emperor Titus took Jerusalem, he ordered the citizens to dump their rubbish daily on what was left of the temple, because so many Romans had been killed there. He wanted the temple covered forever. Later, Sultan Soliman wondered why all the citizens dumped their rubbish there and ordered everyone to clean the rubbish away. They dug for thirty days.

> At last, a long wall was brought to light, the Western Wall (Kotel Maaravi). Then, the Sultan who ruled the city at that time, had thirty men and eight women hung on the Wall and forbade anyone polluting the place in the future. The Sultan then asked the Jews of Jerusalem to rebuild the temple with his financial backing. They refused and said that only God could do it. So the Sultan started to rebuild but never completed it. He also treated the Jews well.

Benjamin also said that no Jew dared venture to tread the pathways leading to the Church of the Sepulcher for fear of his life. This was during his trip in 1847. He also stated that on the Mount of Olives was the tomb of the Prophetess Huldah. Part-

way down the mountains, in a cave, lay the tombs of the Prophet
Samuel and his mother.

Chapter XX

DAVID REUVENI, THE "MESSIAH" (A NON-HERO)

The pages of history recount the tales of many men who have either proclaimed themselves or have been proclaimed as the Messiah. Before the Jeshua of Nazareth (Jesus) and after his time, different men appeared and caused great excitement and aroused millions almost to hysterical joy. One such man was David Reuveni. Here is his story out of the pages of history, not theology.

David Reuveni was born in 1500 C.E., somewhere in Central Europe. He was a dwarf, dark and swarthy in appearance, but commanding a magnetic, spellbinding personality. He became an adventurer and traveled throughout Egypt and Palestine. When he was twenty-four-years-old, he appeared in Venice on a magnificent huge white Arabian steed. The contrast between horse and man alone was enough to startle one into awe. He announced that he was the brother to the king of the tribe of Reuben, one of the lost ten tribes of Israel and that the king had sent him to obtain the help of the Pope (Clement VII) for a "Jewish Crusade" against the Moslems. He stated that he was the commander of thousands of fierce Jewish warriors in Arabia who were ready to do battle. So convincing was he to the Pope that he was granted an audience by the Pope himself. After all, Clement thought, the Messiah had to be a Jew, and think how grand it would look to have Jews fighting, in effect, the battle of Christianity. Pope Clement VII couldn't afford to overlook any bets. Besides, he was having sore troubles with the Protestants, Turks were marching into Europe and who knows what other troubles were plaguing the Church! Besides, the Pope, as many popes before him, was a good war strategist and knew that a Jewish army, any army, attacking the

Turks from the rear (by way of Arabia) would be of tremendous strategic importance. Even the Pope's astrologers gave their okay.

The Pope consulted with the king of Portugal, and he gave his blessing also. The king of Portugal certified him as a diplomatic emissary from a friendly kingdom and backed him financially. By now, even the Jews in Europe as well as the ordinary Christians, were sitting up and taking notice. Maybe Reuveni was the Messiah. After all he could appear as a dwarf or a giant, blonde or swarthy, because the Messiah was capable of many things!

The Pope gave Reuveni a ship flying a Jewish flag (Mogen David) from Italy and he sailed to Portugal. In honor of Reuveni's visit, King John III of Portugal even stopped burning Jews (Marranos) during the talks between him and Reuveni. But the Marranos were so impressed with Reuveni and his power that they publicly started calling him the Messiah. Christians even began converting to Judaism. The king and the priests were becoming perturbed, so Reuveni wisely set sail for Italy. The newly converted Christians were then burned at the stake and the Marranos went into hiding.

In Italy, Diogo Pires, a crypto Christian-Marrano joined Reuveni. Pires was another man who had proclaimed himself Messiah and had preached to the poor, lame, halt, lepers, etc., even to the point that the Pope granted him immunity from the Inquisition. When he had first converted to Judaism, he had changed his name to Solomon Molko. Molko and Reuveni traveled to Ratisbon (now Regensburg), to offer (not ask, mind you) the Emperor Charles V, of the Holy Roman Empire, an alliance against the Turks if he would aid the "King of the Jews in Arabia".

Charles V listened to their story. This Emperor, who neither could read nor write, hated Protestants almost as much as he hated Jews. Here, he had one Jew who proclaimed himself the Messiah (Molko) and another Jew who had half of Europe believing he was the Messiah, although not actually claiming he was. And Reuveni, to boot, was a dwarf and dark skinned, not a tall, blonde, Nordic type!

Charles V put them both in prison and turned them over to the Inquisition. If one of them was the Messiah, he could after all, prove it by freeing himself. Molko was offered the chance to become a Christian, but since he was the "Messiah", he would redeem mankind and be slain again. He was burned at the stake. Reuveni was taken to Spain, where his fate is still in doubt to this day. It is reported that he was burned at the stake, but it also reported that he talked his way out of prison. With his fabulous gift of gab, who knows! No one is sure of his origin and no one is very sure of his fate. The Bodleian Library at Oxford, England contains part of the diary of David Reuveni, the dwarf who awakened Europe for a short time to Messianic expectations.

Chapter XXI
CULTURE IN SAN FRANCISCO

A distinct pattern of immigration of European Jews took place in the 1800s in the United States. The Eastern European Jews settled on the East Coast while the German Jews migrated to the West Coast.

The Russian and Eastern European Jews emigrated out of ghettoes and oppressive countries and settled where they got off the boats. Tending to emigrate separately, breaking up family communities, they often ended up living outside a strong Jewish environment in America.

German and Sephardic Jews, on the other hand, tended to emigrate in entire family groups, usually from small communities. German Jews were more affluent when they emigrated, and a large majority left the East Coast quickly and headed for California. From 1848–50, these settlers found in San Francisco a community that lacked an Establishment. They arrived as venture capitalists during the Gold Rush and instead of taking to the mines they became, or remained, merchants. These Jews brought with them the strong Mediterranean and German cultural tradition and were able to establish it in a more or less German environment in San Francisco. They were the masters of German and Spanish culture. So this vital first generation Jewry made money and became The Establishment. Throughout the 1800s, the San Francisco Jews established an upper class society that has prospered through today. From their Germanic artistic tradition, they became the leaders of San Francisco culture and philanthropy. You can look almost anywhere in San Francisco and see the names of these families, Stern Grove, Steinhart Aquarium, Fleishhaker Zoological Gardens. By most measures, you could term the arrival and establishment of the Jews in San Francisco as the flowering of Jewish Ascendancy.

The San Francisco census for 1860 showed a figure of 380,000, with 21,626 German Jews. Some of these pioneers are Adolph H. Sutro, Levi Strauss, Louis Sloss and Louis Gerstle. There are businessmen like Isaias W. Hellman, Mortimer and Herbert Fleishhaker, and Anthony Zellerback. There are political figures: Abe Reuf, Harris Weinstock, Julius and Florence Kahn, and Sol Bloom; social innovators – David Lubin, Rabbi Jacob Nieto, Judah L. Magnes, Jessica B. Peixotto and Sigmund Danielewicz.

Among writers and artists are Gertrude Stein, Alice B. Toklas, David Belasco, Anne Bremer, Joseph Raphael, Ernest Bloch, Darius Milhaud, Yehudi and Isaac Stern. There are builders and scientists such as Joseph B. Strauss, Joseph Eichler and Albert A. Michelson. Not forgotten are the famous newspaper cartoonist Rube Goldberg, the eccentric Joshua A. "Emperor" Norton, and the great heavyweight Joe Choynski.

Chapter XXII
HANNAH OF NATANIA

There was a sweet little lady on 16 Rechov HaRav Kook, Natania, Israel, who made just about the best gefilte fish and matjes herring in the world. The reason that she could do so would make a best selling novel, one that would capture your mind and attention wholeheartedly, absorbed in what comes next. Space herein only permits me to present a small encapsulation.

In a small city in Russia, Hannah Levani was a real beauty as a young lady. She was courted and married, and her husband became quite successful as a businessman. In fact, he had a small factory. Came the Bolshevik Revolution and then the communist takeover. In time, Hannah and her husband were sent to Siberia, to a labor camp, as befell the fate of many of those who had become merchants and businessmen. In the Pale of Russia this was quite a feat, to make something of yourself.

In the labor camp, everyone had to perform tasks. The men would chop wood, do heavy labor; wait on Russian camp managers, etc. Some had to feed the men. Hannah could cook, so she was put to work cooking. What did this entail? There wasn't much meat but they were four miles from a river. So every morning, while it was still dark, she would hike to the river with a basket, catch fish, carry the load on her head back to the barracks, and make all sorts of fish dishes. Sweet and sour herring, matjes herring, gefilte fish, etc. Her "fish" became known throughout the labor camp.

Hannah and her husband along with the remnants of her family found their way to Israel forty years ago. Her husband's mother and father had a large house (under British rule) in Natania. Her husband died and now Hannah became the proprietor of this house. It has been made into a number of small apartments. Not fancy, but clean. With this, she supported herself. Her daughter's husband was killed in the last war, just before her grandson was born. The house is only two or three blocks from a gorgeous beach on the Mediterranean. Large hotels are built or being built nearby. Across the street is a Reform Synagogue; down the street is the small Hotel Ast. In 1972, I stayed there, as did other Sacramento couples. We had an efficient kitchen where we could make our meals if we desired, a dining room, a bedroom, and a semi-private bath, all for about eight dollars a day. Today, of course, it is more expensive. But it's a dandy place to stay, or operate out of, to see all of Israel. Natania is beautiful, too.

Cantor Wald, Frank and Ruth Vinick, Irv and Anne Levine all stayed there. By the way, Hannah didn't speak too much English, but her daughter does. Hannah only spoke Russian, Yiddish, and Hebrew. She was a sweet, typical Jewish mother. She would bring some fish up to your apartment, or salt, or seltzer in a "schpritzer" bottle to make you feel at home. She is now deceased.

Chapter XXIII

JEWS OF THE CARIBBEAN – CUBA

This is a first of a series of articles on the history of Jewish settlement in the islands of the Caribbean Sea. Most of the information here was gathered by Bernard Postal, journalist and co-author of Jewish tourist guides to the United States and Europe. Rabbi Malcolm Stern did much research work. The American Jewish Archives, under Professor Jacob Rader Marcus, also contributed much data. American Airlines assembled much of the information into a *Tourist Guide for Jews*, because a fantastically large percentage of the tourist trade to the Caribbean comprises Jewish travelers. To all the above we owe thanks.

Many islands under many flags were the stopping places or havens for Jews from anti-Semitism of the Spanish Inquisition and Europe, in general. In fact, only Holland gave unlimited haven, at any time, to Jews. The French, Spanish, British drove them out as well as rebellions by the former slaves. We will first talk about Cuba since it is one of the biggest island governments, and played such an important part in modern Jewish history.

Havana, Cuba, has over one and a half million people, of which the Jewish population is down to 1,500 or so. Prior to Castro, there were 15,000 Jews there. But back to the beginning – Luis de Torres and Alonso de Calle, Marrano (secret Jews) members of Columbus's crew, were the first men to set foot on the island from his expedition. When de Torres found tobacco growing there, he stayed and became a tobacco planter as well as the island's first white resident, and incidentally, the earliest Jewish settler in North or South America, to our knowledge. The Inquisition drove more Jews to Cuba. Hernando Alonso, who came with Cortez in 1571, and helped build the ships Cortez used to conquer Mexico, is reputed to have started the sugar industry there. Alonso died at the stake in Mexico for heresy. From that time, until 1783, religious persecution of Jews because of the Inquisition prevailed. From 1783 to 1823, there was some peace for Jews, but the effect of the Inquisition still prevailed. In fact, public worship of anything but Catholicism was forbidden until 1898, when the island was "liberated" from Spain. During all this time, however, Jewish merchants from the United States, Curaçao, and Jamaica, traded extensively with Cuba and some even had branch offices there.

Some old aristocratic Cuban families boasted of Marrano ancestry. In 1869, a renowned Cuban actress, Delores de Dios-Porta, confessed on her deathbed (in Paris) that she was a born a Jewess. Juan Ellis, in the 1820s, organized an underground movement and later, served with Simon Bolivar.

When the Maine was blown up in 1898, the Secretary of the Navy Board of Inquiry was Adolph Marix, the first Jewish admiral in the USN. Americans, who had served in Cuba during the Spanish American War, were the first Jews to settle permanently as planters, industrialists and corporate representatives. The Balkan Wars (1910–1913) caused another steady stream of Jewish refugees to Cuba. Both the first streetcar line in Havana and the movie industry were started by Jews. From 1924 to 1929, 12,000 Polish and Romanian Jews arrived in Cuba. In the 1930s, 3,000 refugees from Nazism also came.

In 1906, a Reform synagogue was established; in 1914, a Sephardic synagogue; in 1924, an Ashkenazic synagogue. In 1935, the Patronato, a Jewish Community Center, tried to unite the Jews. They built an Ashkenazic synagogue, recreation and cultural facilities, a library and a kosher restaurant.

In 1959, there were 15,000 Jews in Cuba with five synagogues, three day schools, cultural, social and Zionist organizations, a B'nai B'rith Lodge, Yiddish and Spanish newspapers. By 1961, there were 8,000 Jews left. By 1971, only 1,500 remained. The Jews had moved to South America, Puerto Rico, Florida, or Israel. The reason the Jews left at this time was not anti-Semitism, but economics. The five synagogues are still open and functioning, however, as are two day schools and the kosher restaurant.

Cuba has good relations with Israel and permits Zionist activity. Cuban volunteers fought in the 1948 Israeli War of

Independence. Cuba's ambassador to Israel was Jewish. Israeli technicians advised Cuban cattle breeding and citrus growing. The government makes kosher meat available in two kosher butcher shops, pays for upkeep of the Jewish cemetery as well as the shochet (ritual slaughterer).

Chapter XXIV
JEWS OF THE CARIBBEAN – JAMAICA

You've all heard of the poetess, Elizabeth Barrett Browning. Her father was the famed Tyrant of Wimpole Street, Edward Moulton Barrett. When the Jews needed to expand the cemetery, which they had outgrown in 1851, they purchased land from Mr. Barrett at Falmouth, Jamaica. Falmouth is one of the many old Jewish Cemeteries abounding all over Jamaica. They attest to the large Jewish population that Jamaica used to have. The Falmouth Cemetery dates from 1760, but Jewish settlement is considered to have been started in 1530, twenty-one years after the first Spanish settlement or thirty-six years after Columbus discovered Jamaica, according to Richard Hill, a Christian scholar.

Governor de Cordova (1590s) was said to be descended from the Marranos. When the British conquered Jamaica in 1655, about 750 (one half of the white population) were Marrano Jews, or "Portugals", called so because they had escaped the Portuguese Inquisition. A local Marrano (Captain Campoe Sabbatha) guided the British into Kingston Bay. Acosta, also a Jew, was the British supply master who arranged the terms of the Spanish surrender. Every Spaniard was ordered to leave except the Marranos.

After the British took over, the Marranos openly professed Judaism and were granted British citizenship by Oliver Cromwell (twenty-seven years before the Jews of England) and later confirmed by King Charles II. By 1680, refugees from Brazil and colonists from France, Holland, and England arrived, including many Ashkenazim. Port Royal was the first thriving Jewish Community. (The Hunt's Bay Jewish Cemetery was established in the 1660s). The first Jewish Synagogue was started in 1676, at Port Royal, and was decimated by the earthquake of 1692. In 1815, Port Royal itself was wiped out by fire. The Jews then moved to Kingston and Spanish Town. Spanish Town had synagogues since 1704, however. Fires and subsequent earth-quakes ruined many synagogues over the years. The present synagogue, which unites the Ashkenazim, Sephardim, Progressive, etc., is the United Congregation of Israelites or Duke Street Synagogue.

Jewish merchants were doing so well that in 1671, the Christian merchants petitioned for the expulsion of all Jews. These Jewish merchants, by the way, had defended themselves and their goods very well against pirates who teemed all about Jamaica and the Caribbean. The Christian merchants tried again in 1681 but again failed. But a special tax was levied on the Jews so that by 1700, eighty Jewish families bore most of the tax load in Jamaica.

The Jews developed sugar, molasses, vanilla, bauxite, and also other industries. Led by Moses Delgado, in 1831, they obtained all the rights of citizenship and could hold public office. In 1835, Bravo was elected to the Assembly. In 1836, Daniel Hart was the first Jamaican to free his slaves. Hart, Sanguinetti and Barnett also became Assembly men. By 1849, eight of the forty-seven assembly men were Jews. Out of respect for them, offices were closed on Yom Kippur. The newspaper was founded by Jacob de Cordova. Jacob later laid out the city of Waco, Texas. So many Jews were prominent in Jamaica, in the 18th century, that Jamaican almanacs contained Hebrew letters.

In spite of all the above, "intermarriage" between the Ashkenazim and Sephardim was considered almost as bad as marrying a non-Jew. Dr. Lewis Ashenheim married Eliza de Cordova, the first intermarriage of prominence. His grandson, Sir Neville Noel Ashenheim, who helped lead Jamaica to independence in 1962, was first ambassador to the United States, was one of the authors of Jamaica's constitution and boss of the *Daily Gleaner* (newspaper). A recent mayor of Kingston, Eli Matalon, was the second generation of a Syrian Jewish family. The Matalons built part of the new Kingston Harbor and many housing projects. The House of Myers (Myers Rum) is world famous. During World War II, 1,000 German Jewish refugees were taken care of. The Kingston community has several cemeteries, the Jewish Institute, Hillel Academy, a multiracial non-denominational school established by Rabbi Hooker, a B'nai B'rith lodge and a WZO (Women's Zionist Organization), all with about 800 Jews left on Jamaica. Remember, when you hear names like Cordova, Andrade, Morales, Hart, Pereira, Mendes, Diaz, Fernandez, Bravo, da Costa, these were all Jews who played a part in Jamaican history.

Chapter XXV

JEWS OF THE CARIBBEAN – DOMINICAN REPUBLIC

When Columbus landed and named the island Hispaniola, Luis de Torres was the first man ashore. The tree to which he moored his boat and the "ashes of Columbus", are preserved today in Santa Domingo, the capital. Marranos settled here during the reign of Columbus's son Diego, who governed from 1509 to 1520. No trace remains of these early Marranos, although General Marcheva, the Minister of Finance, in the late 1890s, claims to be a descendant, as do many white settlers.

Early in the 19ᵗʰ century, Jews from Curaçao arrived in Santa Domingo. Around 1890, Russian Jews joined them. In 1938, Jewish refugees from Austria and Nazi Germany came to the Dominican Republic. During the Evian Conference, called by President Roosevelt to consider ways of easing the refugees' plight, thirty-one nations including the United States, did nothing. Only the spokesman for Rafael Trujillo, president of the Dominican Republic, announced that the Dominican Republic would admit 100,000 Jews.

Trujillo even gave 26,000 acres at Sosua, his personal property. Sosua was on the Northern coast. Later, Trujillo added two more pieces of land, totaling 53,000 acres. The American Joint Distribution Committee organized the Dominican Republic Settlement Association (DORSA) in 1940. The Dominican Republic then waived all taxes, permitted the settlers to bring in tools and equipment, duty free, and guaranteed them freedom of religion. By 1941, 413 people arrived, eventually to grow to 670. Each settler was given seventy acres, ten cows and some money from Agro-Joint (a defunct US society for Russian Jewish farmers). No one had experience in farming or manual trades.

DORSA spent $3,000,000 on transportation, land, improvement, roads, housing and maintenance before the settlers became self-sufficient. Dairy farms and cattle breeding flourished. A hospital, school, synagogue and radio station was established. Alfred Rosenzweig, Sosua's managing director, was elected to the Dominican Republic Senate in 1951.

By the mid 50s, young people began to leave for Puerto Rico, United States, and Israel. Some of the Jews married native women and were rearing their children as Catholics. By 1966, the Jewish Population was 200 (56 families). Today, it is even less. During World Refugee Year (1959–60), the Dominican Republic issued two stamps depicting the Jewish Colony at Sosua and its people. Today, there are 175 people in Sousa, twelve in Santiago, and about 150 in Santo Domingo; two synagogues, a Jewish school, and an Israeli embassy.

Even before Sosua was established, Santo Domingo had a flourishing Jewish community. From 1939 to 1946, a newspaper (*Diario de Sabado*) was published in Spanish, Yiddish and German. A split in the community between the Yiddish and German-speaking elements led to the formation of a new group. In 1957, a modern synagogue, entirely financed by Trujillo was opened, and the rift healed somewhat. Trujillo was indeed true to his word about complete freedom for Jews. A number of refugees from Germany lived in the Dominican Republic before they eventually moved to the United States.

Chapter XXVI

JEWS OF THE CARIBBEAN – PUERTO RICO

Puerto Rico (PR) has over 2,000 Jews, the largest number in the Caribbean, most of whom are located in San Juan. In addition, there are B'nai B'rith, Hadassah, United Synagogue Youth, and Sisterhoods of the synagogues and about a half dozen delis or restaurants.

We don't know much about old synagogues or very early settlers, except for the belief that Jews from the Balearic Islands moved to PR about 1519. Columbus, of course, discovered PR on his second voyage to the Western Hemisphere and naturally on this trip he carried Marranos. The reason we don't have much early Jewish settlement is because of the Inquisition. Some of Teddy Roosevelt's Rough Riders were Jewish, according to United States Army records. Some of the US contingent settled in PR and helped establish a congregation at Ponce, in 1899. From 1900 to 1920, no established community existed. Charles Gans, of Connecticut, opened a cigar factory. Those Jews who couldn't get into the US because of the 1924 immigration quota, moved to PR to await admittance to the United States. Two of these, Simon Benus and Aaron Levine, stayed on to build up a chain of department stores. In 1900, Leo Stanton Rowe was appointed to codify PR's laws. He later became president of the Pan American Union. Jacob Hollander organized the island's revenue system, as the first treasurer of PR. Louis Suzbacher was a justice of PR's first supreme court. Adolph Wolf succeeded him. Dr. Julius Matz headed the island's pathology lab at Rio Piedras. Joseph Jacobs was instrumental in developing the islands first irrigation system. The list of names goes on and on.

In 1917, there were only six Jewish families registered in the

Pan American Union trade report; in 1927, expanding to twenty-six families; by 1942, thirty-eight families. However, when thousands of US troops poured into PR in World War II, the Jewish population exploded to over 300 with all sorts of organizations. (Get ten Jews together and you'll get eleven organizations). The post-war tax breaks induced US businessmen to settle there, and also started a tourist boom in the 1950s. The Jews came as engineers, factory and plant managers, entrepreneurs and teachers. After the Cuban revolution, 150 more families moved to PR to become prominent in retail trades and provided doctors.

In 1953, a Jewish Community Center and a synagogue were started in the same old mansion. B'nai B'rith organized a lodge in 1964. The reform temple was started in 1967. At last report, the community was still growing. If it weren't for the influence of the Inquisition, there might have been many thousands of Jews there. But again, as history has shown us, only the Dutch had an unblemished record for full freedom for Jews. (Oh yes, Peter Stuyvesant was severely reprimanded by Holland for his overt anti-Semitism.)

Chapter XXVII
JEWS OF THE CARIBBEAN –
CURAÇAO

The Dutch have almost always held out a hand of welcome to the Jews. And, so it was in what is now the independent Netherlands Antilles. Curaçao is the largest of six islands in this group, the other two main ones being Bonaire and Aruba. Willemstad, the capital had 65,000 people, now has less than 1,000 Jews. But now let's retrace the pages of history.

Samuel Cohen, a Portuguese Marrano, was interpreter on a Dutch ship in 1634. He spoke Dutch, Portuguese, Spanish and Indian dialects and was active when the Dutch fleet captured Curaçao from the Spanish. He looked for gold, in vain and moved back to Amsterdam. He left Julio de Aranjo, another Marrano who didn't stay long either. But every Dutch ship carried Jews seeking haven from the Inquisition. In 1651, the Dutch West India Company issued a proclamation inviting settlement there. Joao de Yllan, another ex-Marrano, led twelve Jewish settlers (out of fifty who had promised to go) there, but they didn't stay long because farming was unprofitable. In 1659, Isaac da Costa led seventy Jews from Amsterdam to Curaçao and they established a permanent colony. In 1659, Congregation Mikve Israel was founded after a small group had been meeting since 1651.

With the development of the slave trade, Curaçao prospered and by 1776 there were about 2,000 Jews. The synagogue had outgrown its first building and had a new one built in 1732 (it's still standing). The ordinances developed by the shul (synagogue) members governed the islands' Jews for about 200 years. Of course, many factions broke away, new shuls were started and bitter divisions afflicted the community. It got so bad, the governor of the island was called upon to make peace.

B'nai B'rith and BBYO flourished. There is a women's International Zionist Organization, a Jewish delicatessen and a book store. The Maduro family played a leading role in commerce and industry, creating a deep inland harbor and a port with facilities. This family also served as bankers, brokers and agents for Shell Oil and KLM. Other Jews pretty much controlled trade and dominated the professions. They have always had close ties with Israel. Tourism, especially for Jews, is a big deal there too.

I lived in Curaçao for about six months during World War II. The people were very friendly and tried to marry me off to their daughters. Talk about being strict – you were constantly chaperoned! I loved the climate, the sea breezes and all the languages that were spoken including Papiamento, the jargon of Indian, Spanish, Dutch, and you name it. Fact is, I believe I still owe five dollars to my half-black/half-Indian laundry woman for cleaning my navy whites. I was shipped out on very short notice on a ship bound for the Mediterranean. I really missed those Rum and Coca Colas (Cuba libras) for quite a while afterwards. My wife and I plan to visit Curaçao to celebrate the 350th anniversary of the synagogue. Chaim Potok, the author will speak and twenty-five cantors will sing in chorus, all to celebrate the oldest synagogue in the Western Hemisphere.

Chapter XXVIII

CURAÇAO – A JEWISH HAVEN

The time: 1943 and 1944. The place: Curaçao of the Netherlands Antilles in the Caribbean. During WWII, Aruba and Curaçao were the only places providing oil to the US. Royal Dutch Shell Company, having a large refinery there, and German submarines were sinking tankers and trying to torpedo the refinery. I was stationed there as part of the US Navy detachment. The islanders were very hospitable and gracious.

On April 20, 2001, I returned to Curaçao for the 350th anniversary of Temple Mikve Israel Emanuel (MIE), the oldest continually operating synagogue in the Western Hemisphere. On April 21, my wife Sylvia and I went to the synagogue for Sabbath services and met Mr. Rene D. L. Maduro, the synagogue president. I gave him a letter from Rabbi Brad Bloom, authorizing me as Sacramento Congregation B'nai Israel's representative to the occasion, a congratulatory letter stating that the oldest synagogue west of the Mississippi salutes and honors Temple MIE, and a two foot by three foot poster commemorating Congregation B'nai Israel's 150 years seniority. Mr. Maduro and others loved the poster and thanked me for the letter. We then took part in the service, which was Sephardic, originating in Portugal.

Curaçao was a Dutch possession since 1634. Holland has always been liberal to all religions, and Jews there held high positions. A number of Jewish families went to Amsterdam to escape the inquisition in Portugal. Then, ten or twelve of these families went to Curaçao to make a new life on a Dutch island. More Jews followed. The number of Jews increased to 3,500 at one time. They brought commerce, banking, shipping, maritime insurance and shipmasters to Curaçao. At one time, their capital, Willemstad, had twice the shipping tonnage of New York City. At one time, more than half of the white population was Jewish. Curaçao is now ninety percent black. All inhabitants speak four languages: Dutch, English, Spanish and Papiamento. Papiamento has a number of Hebrew and Portuguese words attributed to Jewish influence.

Temple Mikve Israel was very affluent, and by the end of the 18th century, the Jewish community was the wealthiest and most important in the Western Hemisphere. They helped other synagogues get started: the Touro Synagogue in Rhode Island; the Shearith Israel Congregation in New York City; the synagogue in Charleston, S. C.; Kingston, Jamaica; St. Eustatius, Netherlands Antilles; St. Thomas, Virgin Islands; Paramaribo, Surinam and Colon, Panama. In fact, the Touro and New York synagogues offer a special prayer every Yom Kippur for the Curaçao community.

In 1864, a group broke away from Temple Mikve Israel to form Temple Emanuel, a more liberal congregation. After a hundred years, Rabbi Maslin convinced both synagogues to merge and now the synagogue was called Temple Mikve Israel Emanuel. They call themselves Reconstructionists, but I believe they are conservative – you cannot daven (pray) unless you wear a talit and kipa. The service is Sephardic. Rabbi Tayvah wears a three-cornered Portuguese hat, and the president wears a top hat for important functions.

Everyone bows before mounting the stairs to the ark that holds the Torahs. Believe it or not, on Tuesday the 22nd, when the whole community celebrated the anniversary, they read from a Torah that was 680 years old – from the year 1320. The Catholic cardinal, the head of the Protestant Church, Prince William representing his mother (Queen Beatrix, the queen of Holland), the prime minister, governor and other notables were present as well as part of the entire Curaçaon community.

The synagogue has ten black families, but many more visit. There is absolutely no anti-Semitism. In fact, nineteen streets are named after Jews. There are large statues of some Jews like an earlier prime minister, Da Costa Gomez. During the 1800s, the slaves revolted against the Dutch landowners, but not against Jewish landowners. Not many Jews had slaves or were in the slave business.

The first Jewish cemetery Beth Chaim, which was established in 1659, has 5,000 graves. Some gravestones have skull and crossbones on them signifying pirates, we were told. There is now another new cemetery – only a hundred years old. There is an orthodox Ashkenazic synagogue with a hundred families, but we did not get an opportunity to see it.

BBYO youth put on a puppet show which was simply marvelous! One puppet wore a kipa, a talit, had a white beard, and held a Torah. He told the history of the Jews of Curaçao while other puppets in the background acted out his statements. There are now seventeen or so youth in BBYO and sixty-four men in the B'nai B'rith Lodge.

According to our guide, the supermarkets are run by Portuguese, the restaurants mostly by Chinese, the furniture stores by Arabs, and the car dealers, banks, shipping and insurance by Jews. Curaçao liqueur was started by a Jewish family named Senior. They used orange peels and spices to achieve the various flavors. Orange crops never really matured in Curaçao, as agriculture was not a successful business due to the rocky terrain. Most produce comes from Venezuela, which is thirty-five miles to the south. Every morning a fleet of small boats arrives with fresh produce.

There is a Jewish museum that has many interesting items including a table set for Pesach from the 1600s and later. Twenty-two cantors performed before a crowd of 2,000. Three cantors performed solos also. It was really an event to behold! I am supplying a list of the cantors and their locations to the Voice and Temple B'nai Israel. Chaim Potok, the author, spoke before another immense crowd. He is also a Rabbi, a painter and a poet.

There was an art exhibit as well as a photography exhibit. The photographs were of synagogues of Venezuela and the Caribbean. The photos were expanded to two feet by three feet without losing contrast or definition. Rabbi Pynchas Brener of Caracas organized the expedition to obtain the photographs. He spoke to an assembly of visitors who came to Curaçao for the anniversary. Among the visitors were rabbis and cantors galore as well as people who had ties to Curaçao.

The weather was perfect! Trade winds kept down the humidity. It was a pleasure both day and night. There are seventy beaches; the best ones were on the southern coast. Some information that really surprised me: Caracas Venezuela has 3,500 Jewish families and twelve synagogues; Jamaica now has one (there were two in the capital) with 300 families; Aruba forty-five families; Costa Rica 2,500 Jews with 500 families of which sixty-five families are Reform. Panama City has 5,000 Jews and four synagogues. There are synagogues in Surinam (Dutch Guinea), Barbados, Coro (Venezuela) and others. I have a list of thirty Jewish family names that are Latino like Lopez, Valencia, Chaves, Da Costa, Gomez, Cardozo, Redondo, etc.

Curaçao now has less that 400 Jews as most of the young who have gone to the States or Europe for their education have not returned, except to visit. The family unit consists of one or two in most cases. Many Europeans vacation there while most US folks go to Aruba, which is the island next door. We will always cherish our visit to Curaçao.

Chapter XXIX

JEWS OF THE CARIBBEAN – ST. THOMAS

Most of you have heard of Charlotte Amalie capital city, as a free port where you can get fabulous deals duty-free on merchandise from all over the world. There were about 200 Jews there four years ago, and it is now believed that there are about 400. The reform synagogue (B'racha V' Shalom V' Gemilath Chasidim) was built in 1833, after a previous synagogue was blown away by a hurricane. Since the oldest Jewish Cemetery bears inscriptions from 1792 and later, many claim that Jews were here before Curaçao. There are two Jewish restaurants. You can even get kosher food at hotels if you notify them in advance. Jewish tourism is quite high. The one claim to fame is that of the birthplace of Camille Pissarro (1830–1903), a famous French Jewish impressionist.

General

In 1781, British Admiral Rodney raided St. Eustatius Island because its residents were supplying arms to the colonies. The merchants, most of them Jews, fled to St. Thomas and St. Croix, where they prospered for a while under Danish rule. In 1801, there were nine families listed. By 1850, 800 Jews (half of the white population) were in St. Thomas. When steamships replaced sailing ships, the island's economy went downhill, helped along by cholera and a hurricane. By 1890, there were only 140 Jews left. In 1907, when the United States purchased the islands, there were only forty Jews and a rabbi was the only clergyman on all of the islands.

David Levy Yulee, the first Jew elected to the US Senate (1845

Florida) and Judah P. Benjamin, Secretary of State of the Confederacy were born in St. Thomas. Morris de Castro was made governor by President Truman in 1950. The Levy and Paiewonsky families came to St. Thomas in 1880s and became the leaders of the islands' economic, cultural and political life. You might say that St. Thomas was ruled by the Jews before Israel was. The Paiewonskys founded a college, the B'nai B'rith Lodge and other activities there. President Kennedy appointed Ralph Paiewonsky as territorial governor in 1961. He encouraged tourism and made the islands the famous tourist center it is today. Most of the Jews there now are from the United States. Herman Wouk also lived there.

Chapter XXX

JEWS OF THE CARIBBEAN – ST. CROIX

St. Croix can lay claim to only a handful of Jews and a cemetery dating from 1779, but it has had Jewish governors and famous Jewish families that go back to the 1600s. In 1684, Gabriel Moran, a Jewish soldier of fortune, governed all three islands for Denmark. Moran was a scoundrel, however, and was recalled to Copenhagen and hanged. In 1685, a contract dealing with importing of slaves, also mentioned that Jews and Catholics could hold services in private, provided they caused no scandals. Benjamin and Emanuel Voss were shipowners. Moses Henrigues was a fiscal agent for ships going from St. Thomas to Glückstadt in the 1680s. In 1733, France gave up St. Croix to Denmark. In 1700, a small congregation had formed at Christinstad, which lasted a hundred years. Moses Benjamin imported kosher meat from New York City.

Chapter XXXI
THE KABALA

The Kabala was responsible for sprouting new religions, creeds, sects and a fantastic interest in things Jewish by non-Jewish people. To this day, the Kabala is devoutly read, worshipped and followed by people of many faiths in many countries. The Kabala, which glorified in the "exalted presence of God", was authored and elaborated upon by men throughout the last 1,600 years. Prophecy, Zoroastrian mythology, Greek science, numerology, mysticism, and much of metaphysics have the Kabala as its origin. The *Book of Formation,* which appeared in the 8th century really created fantastic interest and zeal in Kabala. The "Zohar" in the 13th century, fanned this zeal into all sorts of philosophical directions. The Zohar, or Book of Splendor is a commentary on the Torah and concerns Jewish mysticism and metaphysics.

Many Kabbalists, who delved into the numerology and mysticism, were responsible for developing new concepts in science. As we reported earlier, Ibn Daud, a Jew in the Arabian Empire, was considered responsible for the concept of Zero and its introduction into European mathematics in the early 1200s. In the 12th century, Abraham bar Hiyya translated Greek and Arabic scientific methodology. Around 1250, Abraham Ibn Latif combined Kabbalism, Aristotelianism, math and natural science into a unified system. A French Jew, Immanuel Bonfils, mathematician and astronomer, is credited with inventing the decimal system in the 14th century. Now, this is 150 years before European scientists accepted it. In the 14th century, Levi ben Gerson introduced a new trigonometric system because of the faulty methodology and results achieved using what then existed. Trigonometry of today is based on Gerson's system.

All of these accomplishments were achieved before the inventions of the microscope, the telescope, the thermometer and the accurate clock. Do you realize what this means? The concept, the rationalization, the theory came before the means to measure such concepts quantitatively.

Chapter XXXII

THE TALMUD

Why do we hear so many references to the Talmud? What is it? Who wrote it? What does it mean to you – a Jew – living in modern times, in a supposedly enlightened populace?

Many Christians, ignorant of Talmudic writings, over the years have damned it as a secret doctrine, a plan to rule the world, a document deliberately kept from the Christian world. You can read it all "Online" electronically, for all the world to see.

To answer all the questions posed above, in a thorough manner, would take a vast amount of time. Herewith, in a nutshell, so to speak, is an attempt to provide some answers.

The Talmud is an open book, or a compilation of books (sixty-three volumes), or a collection of hundreds of men's clarification of the writings in the Torah – open to anyone, who wants to read it, in at least a few dozen languages. It was started about 400 years before the Common Era (400 B.C.E.).

The Torah, the first five books of the Bible, was considered complete about 450 years before the Common Era and was "canonized" by Ezra and Nehemiah in Jerusalem. These writings were in Hebrew. Because of the complexity and the number of statutes (613) contained therein, many men were seeking explanations. And so the Midrash (sermons) was started.

Scholars gathered and unofficially rendered interpretations of Mosaic Law. After 200 years, the Mishnah was started – an official attempt to collate all the unofficial interpretations. The Mishnah was divided into Halacha (the Law) and the Haggadah (the Narration or Discussion). This lasted for 200 years up until about 200 C.E.

In Palestine and Babylonia, scholars began methodically reinterpreting all that had proceeded. Most of the writings (called the Gemara) were rendered in Aramaic, the commonly spoken language of the times, but still some of the more exacting interpretations were written in Hebrew. To the Halacha was added the Midrash (sermons). Of the two Gemaras, the Babylonian was considered intellectually superior and developed over 300 years. In Babylonian universities, Talmudic knowledge was disseminated for another 600 years. Incidentally, the heads of these universities were called "Gaonim" one of the most famous being Saadya Gaon.

In France, around 1100 C.E., Rashi made the first reinterpretation of the Talmud again in Hebrew. His children and grandchildren (known as the Tosaphot) carried on his work. Bear in mind that during all the years, many men with new thinking, new ideas, built upon the past, brought in the present and left room for future growth and change. This means that Judaism was – and is – an ever changing, living, always modern concept of law, ethics, and morals, which I believe to be one of the reasons for its survival. We are not a stagnant, archeological relic living on past glories, as Toynbee would have us believe.

We are ever building. Your son may be one of these who add to the Commentary.

To go on with history… at the same time that Rashi was writing in France, Rabbi Alfasi in Fez, North Africa, codified the Talmud in Hebrew. Fez, at one time, was a large center of Jewish population. About 1200 C.E., the Talmud was recodified (Mishnah Torah) by Rambam (Rabbi Moses ben Maimon, commonly called Maimonides) in Cordoba, Spain, also in Hebrew. About 1600 C.E., Rabbi Joseph Caro from Toledo, Spain wrote the third main codification (Schulchan Aruch), in Palestine, also in Hebrew. Much has been written by famous men since then, like Spinoza, Buber and others but no more significant changes have been made to the Talmud.

It seems rather ironic that in Iraq, where so much Jewish history unfolds, where so much enlightenment and culture was manifest, Jews are treated now – like dogs. At Nehardea, Pumbedita, and Sura, three great universities made the Babylonian Talmud a reality. From Babylonia, the word was sent to Jews in Egypt, Greece, Italy, Spain, France, and Germany – where the Talmud made the Jews a universal people wherever they happened to reside. With the Torah as the means of carrying out its intent, the Jews have lived as a civilized society even where no civil law existed.

Chapter XXXIII

A TREATISE ON THE TALMUD

> By three things is the world sustained: by the law, by labor, and by doing righteousness...
>
> Be of an exceedingly humble spirit, for the end of man is the worm...

The above maxims are two of many that are found in *Pirke Abot* (Ethics of the Fathers), a part of the Talmud. For centuries, wise men analyzed and distilled each portion of the Torah, and while doing so commented on life itself, its foibles, its tragedies, its joys and the relationship of one life to another. These commentaries are as true today as they were then.

The Talmud is an archive of debate and dialogue, starting in both the Babylonian and Palestinian academies, of the interpretation of the Torah and the development of Jewish law and tradition. Yes, the tradition we have been living by, is derived from fifteen centuries of continuous dialogue. You, the present day Jew, are a result of that dialogue, whether you realize it or not.

All the previous discussions and decisions rendered in the past were carried down by continuous debate, distilling, reinterpreting and building. Due to the Talmud we are more than a "religion". We are an ethical body, a moral conscience, and a legislated nation. Because of the Talmud, the meanings of the Torah were explained to the people, and these meanings were issued as statutes. In the main, the punishments for deviation from these statutes were moral guilt for performing an injustice, or fear of being ostracized or outcast from the community.

Back to the Talmud. Because so much has been written explaining the Bible, the only way to tell you what is written is to tell you some of what is written.

A. A man may betroth a woman by his own act or by that of an agent.

B. A man may give his daughter in betrothal while she is a Na'arah (that is, twelve years, six months and one day minimum age. In other words, when puberty sets in). Then,

C. One may not give his daughter in betrothal while she is a minor but wait until she grows up and says, "I want Mr. __."

So you see how we develop from A to B to C.

"One is not permitted to work more than a day's journey from his domicile unless he obtains his wife's permission; for one has a responsibility to his wife..." and we talk of "woman's lib" as news!

There are sixty-three treatises, organized under six divisions. SEEDS concerns agriculture and things pertaining thereto. SPECIALLY APPOINTED DAYS concerns Sabbath, Holidays, fasts, etc. WOMEN concerns relations between men and women, marriage, divorce. DAMAGES concerns civil law, criminal law, courts. HOLY THINGS deals with temple ritual, slaughter of animals, eating of animal food. PURITIES deals with ceremonial impurities, etc.

Rabbi Akiba, in the 2nd century, organized the interpretations and traditions that were handed down to him into a systematic body of law. He also used specific cases as precedent to establish general law. Our rabbis have traditionally been lawyers and jurists, which, I guess, is why we are called the "People of the Book".

One last saying that is worthy of note.

Let all those who labor in behalf of the community engage in such work for the sake of Heaven, guiding people along an upright course, restraining them from evil ways, reproving them when necessary. Their objective must not be self-aggrandizement, acquiring honor, wealth, power or pride: for a public figure who lords it over the community is despised by God.

Chapter XXXIV
THE GREAT PRETENDERS

BY ALLAN GROSSMAN – PARIS, FRANCE
(1917–1996)

When Hitler achieved power in 1933, he contrived the world's first concentration camp near Munich, Germany. He confined thousands of political and non-Aryan opponents by concentrating them in a strange campsite. Dachau became the baby and mother of all death camps. Like the calendar year, it became the sole parent of 365 subsidiary and dominant concentration camps throughout central Europe. Himmler, the Munich police chief, was initially in charge. The dreadful Eichmann and Mengele joined his staff in unimaginable destruction. A special camp was erected nearby for the unmerciful "SS" elite Nazi troops. During its twelve years of existence, Dachau was a notorious institution of learning where its pupils developed talent for extermination, torture, genocide and barbarous medical experiments. It became "the killing fields" of Europe.

The Nazis made the Holocaust their "holy cause". "The Final Solution", geared to exterminate Jewry, not only in Europe, but also throughout the world, was established in 1942. Millions were voluminously subdued in large-scale genocide, while the world attached little attention. Finally, the disastrous reputation of Dachau erupted with its monstrous atrocities.

After a relentless drive across Germany, the American Army liberated Dachau on April 29, 1945. On that memorable day, I penetrated Dachau. I perceived we Americans were morally unprepared for this rare event. Although our government was cognizant about the authenticity of the extermination camps, the Holocaust never made front-page news back home. It was the only camp where the weak inmates rebelled before being liberated. We had liberated prisoner of war camps, but this was our first encounter with a wholesale death camp. The experience subjected us to a shock treatment.

I recall conversing in English and Yiddish with some relieved inmates. I was perplexed when they inquired why it took so long to liberate them. The astonishing guided tour of the camp petrified me. The spectacle of the gas chambers, human incinerators, the living skeletons barely able to walk, the unbearable stench, and the mute prisoners were horribly repulsive. I recall the pyramid of thousands of discarded shoes and clogs left behind by the condemned men, women and children, visualizing what poor souls wore the decrepit footwear. Verifying this spectacle so difficult to believe, I wondered if my eyes were betraying me. Desiring to feed the hungry inmates, we contributed our own food rations. A feeling of guilt overcame us the next day when medics claimed some had died during the night because their feeble bodies could not support the "excessive" food. Unaware, humans could stoop so low, I witnessed man's outright inhumanity to man.

Later, we advanced into Czechoslovakia, where we encountered the Russian allied troops. The war in Europe terminated a week after. Somehow, the horrendous impact of Dachau never entirely left me. Forgive, we may, but never forget. If we discard the dreadful past, we are surely condemned to repeat it in the future.

In America and even Paris, I'm confronted with different nationalities asserting that such camps never existed, insisting it's sheer propaganda. With all of their disreputable diatribe, pretensions, denunciation of the truth, some deriving gain for their deceptive support, one can admonish these deranged crackpots as "The Great Pretenders".

BETTER LATE THAT NEVER: It could be The Barcelona Olympics, the world's Fair in Seville, or The Columbus Quincentennial, but I frankly admire King Juan Carlos I of Spain for his bold, candid apology concerning the infamous, repressive Spanish Inquisition and its deadly aftermath commencing in 1492.

We applaud and honor the commendable, authentic French

Resistance Movement during the Second World War. When will France have the courage to admit its guilt for Vichy's intolerant regime and to legally condemn the French leaders responsible for the disgraceful contribution to "The Final Solution"? Must France also wait 500 years?

Chapter XXXV

CAPTIVATING CARPENTRAS

BY ALLAN GROSSMAN PARIS, FRANCE
(1917–1996)

A bewailing cry bellowed through the serene night air of Carpentras. "They killed our dead!"

Over two thousand years ago, Jews of the small provincial sun-swept town of Carpentras flourished in this area before it became part of France. Despite wars, crusades, revolutions, uprisings, pogroms, persecution and anti-Semitism, they managed to prosper in this community. A little over 1,000 Jews, compressed here in 168 homes, formed one of Europe's first walled ghettos. From nearby Avignon, where the Pope governed in 1326, Jews were compelled to wear a yellow Star of David webbed over their heart. The Nazis remembered. The men wore large yellow hats until the French revolution when the color changed to black. Facing city hall, the town had one of the oldest, most beautiful synagogues in Europe. The city recorded its first pogrom in 1459. The clergy seemed to be haunted in its weird method in converting others. Every Saturday, their Sabbath day of rest, Jews were obliged to congregate in the community hall to endure a specific clerical lecture. Many preferred to stuff their ears with wax to avoid verbal indoctrination while others cracked or ate nuts to muffle the orator. An armed guard was always on duty to club anyone slumbering during the sermon. If a Jew openly opposed one's conversion to the church, he was confined to hard labor while his property and possessions were confiscated. The oppressive city officials did not dawdle over such matters. Surprisingly, two years before the revolution, King Louis XVI proclaimed the Edict of Tolerance in 1787, which abolished this unmerciful practice.

The resplendent tree-lined Jewish cemetery of Carpentras, dating from the 14th century, became one of the most renowned in Europe. Many from America and Europe still express their desire to be buried here. Like the city, its cemetery retained a magnetic attraction in spite of its intolerant past. Yet, the brother of the ill-fated Captain Alfred Dreyfus, of the notorious Dreyfus Case, became mayor of Carpentras for twenty-nine years. This provincial town evidently had more to offer than others.

Throughout the dark and middle ages, their cemetery never endured any sign of disrespect or upheaval. Early in May, about ten years ago, the dead were sadistically profaned. Thirty-four graves were severely damaged. A marble grave marker exceeding a ton was shifted and crushed. A recently buried corpse was exhumed, mutilated and scornfully impaled on an umbrella, surmounting the tombs. The living were frequently molested in the past, but this was the first time the dead were profaned and desecrated during their eternal slumber. This particularly abject crime became a bitter message for the living.

Early, during the German occupation of France, young Nathalie Levy fled Paris to hide in the South. When procuring a false national identity card, she changed her name to Leclerc. Like others in her category who survived the occupation, Nathalie was permitted to legally acquire her adopted name, which appeared more accommodating for her. It was similar to Marcel Bloch, the famous French plane constructor, who changed his name to Dassault. Nathalie remained Leclerc for forty-five years. With the contaminated Carpentras desecration, she decided to return to her former name. In mid May, a massive, silent protest manifestation comprising over 200,000 of diverse nationalities was held in Paris. The French president, major political leaders and numerous religious organizations participated, some from the heart and some for political recuperation. Many, not only Jews, wore the symbolic Star of David over their heart. They stood up to be counted. In harmony with the Great Synagogue of Paris, the bells of Notre Dame tolled in protest. The country's massive reaction was consoling. The silent four-hour march made "a big noise" on an international level. My family and I were particularly proud to march along with a certain Nathalie Levy.

Chapter XXXVI
NO MID-EAST MAQUIS

BY MICHEL PIERRE D' ORLEANS – NEW YORK

As one of the principal members of the French resistance against the Nazis, I am shocked to hear the Arabs compare our movement to their terrorist acts against unarmed civilians.

First, France and the rest of the European countries invaded by Nazi Germany never intended to liquidate Germany as the Arabs intend to liquidate Israel. We fought like men against the German army. We never murdered children and women. We never attacked planes carrying innocent passengers. Theirs is not a resistance movement. It is cowardice.

The Arabs are always complaining about the refugees. During the last twenty years, 4,500,000 European people were forced out of the Arab countries. Some 2,200,000 Italians left Libya and Egypt. And 1,700,000 French left Algeria, Tunisia and Morocco. Over 700,000 Jews left Iraq, Yemen, Egypt, Libya, and the other Arab countries. Four and a half million Jews, who had lived in these countries for countless generations, left everything behind. The Arabs took everything. The people left only with the clothes on their backs.

The Arabs had an opportunity to place the 700,000 Arab refugees from Palestine in the homes of the European people who fled the Arab countries. Instead, the refugees were put in camps that cost millions of dollars, contributed by the nations of the world. This was the most brutal thing the Arabs did against their own people.

Palestine was never an Arab country. It never had an Arab government. Palestine had been occupied, since the time of Caesar, by Greeks, Romans, English, and other nations. The only legal government in Palestine was the Jewish government over

2,000 years ago.

The Western World has never understood how the Arab countries, with eighty-five per cent of their population illiterate, millions without jobs, disease and sickness rampant, could spend billions of dollars on ammunition to liquidate a little country like Israel, instead of using the money to build schools, hospitals, homes and industry for their own people.

Chapter XXXVII
TRIPOLI

Years ago, Tripoli (in Libya) was a large commercial town whose population consisted mostly of Moslems. There were 1,000 Jewish families looked over by four Chachamin (prominent rabbis). There were eight synagogues, which fared well under Turkish rule. These synagogues had teachers in Hebrew and Italian. The Nassi of the community (Rabbi Shalom Titu), a rich and learned man, was held in high esteem by the Turkish Pasha, as well as both the Jewish and Christian communities. He, along with a partner, carried on considerable commerce with Sudan. He imported goods from France and Italy and bought dyes and ivory from Arab caravans. The Arabs had perfect confidence in him and desired his opinion on business matters.

Another Rabbi was broker to the French Consul. Still another Rabbi had an extensive Yeshiva and two wives. The community had another Rabbi, for the relief of the poor, and he managed the funds of the community. Each merchant gave five percent of his weekly profit for this purpose. The Jews were permitted to live anywhere in Tripoli. Many Jews held government appointments in the Custom House. The women were dressed quite fashionably and wore makeup.

The climate was not good and many inhabitants suffered from several eye diseases. One-fifth of the population had this problem, in fact, a tenth of the total population was blind. Dates, fruits, and wine grapes, were grown. There were dozens of synagogues within an hour's journey from Tripoli. The only problem the Jews had, was the fanaticism of many Arabs. The Turkish Moslems had more respect for the Jews.

Chapter XXXVIII
THE ORIGIN OF CHRISTIANITY

There are many households where the children or one child took over the rule of that household or where a subsidiary overshadowed the parent corporation; or a small island (Britain) ruled vast countries (India, parts of Africa, etc.). What happens when such an occurrence takes place? If the child is wiser and is also diplomatic, it may be good even though an unhealthy situation. If the subsidiary is building on a "house of cards", again, it is not healthy. If the small country rules for the benefit of its possessions as well as its own people it may be all right, but true freedom is not a reality for its possessions.

What happens when a sect or a small minority of a religious faith attempts to make itself dominant over the father religion? Such is the case vis-à-vis Christianity and Judaism. What happened in this case has been recorded by many historians based on documents; records and actions that to this day make their impact.

From the beginning of the Common Era (about 35 C.E.) until the 4th or 5th century, Christianity was busy deciding what it really was. To make it something unique, it had to rest on its own history and background. The trouble with this thought, though, was that its origins were almost all Jewish (I say origins, not later developments). It had the appearance of a reform movement within Judaism rather, than a new and distinct religion. Judaism was a legally recognized religion by the Romans, and the Jews were free to practice their own customs, ceremonies, etc., without interference; yes, even to govern themselves pretty much as the Sanhedrin and/or the Rabbinical Courts (Bet Din).

To the Romans, the Christians represented another Jewish sect, and if the Christians wished to practice their own ceremonies, they had to do so as Jews practicing Jewish customs.

So, as a result, some people oscillated back and forth between Judaism and Christianity not realizing much difference between the two.

The proponents of a new idea or a new organization have to have something interesting, something of note, and something different to attract adherents. And so there started speeches, arguments, debates until the proponents of those who believed that Jesus was the Christ (Christus from the Greek meaning savior or leader) or the Messiah, started to claim that only they inherited the "Chosen People" claim or prophecy. These "Christian Jews" also claimed that the other Jews refuted the Chosen People inheritance by refusing to accept Jesus as the Messiah. Furthermore, Jesus' death made the other Jews guilty of deicide (killing of God); no punishment was too extreme, God would always hate them, they believed in devils, they would have no salvation, etc. – all because they, the mainstream of Judaism including most all of the Jews, did not accept Jesus as a "God".

This rhetoric became very vitriolic, especially in the sermons of St. John Chrysostom (4th century). He is probably one of the founders of most of the anti-Semitic fables, beliefs and other poppycock. He is still quoted today. Thus, with hate-mongers like St. John Chrysostom and others, anti-Semitism was invented and built into Christianity. The Gospels as written by men after the time of Jesus, started the New Testament with many errors in translation, semantics and jaundiced viewpoints. Whether one was a Judean, Samaritan, Galilean, Idumean, or what have you, he was called a Jew (Judean) in many parts of the New Testament.

When in the 4th century (325 C.E.), Emperor Constantine accepted Christianity as the religion of the Roman Court, this gave official blessing to physical acts of violence, murder, etc., by these Christians against those stubborn Jews who still awaited the coming of the Messiah. What made Constantine accept Christianity for the Roman Empire? The Christians supported him with many men in battle against Lycinius of the Byzantine or Eastern Empire who was trying to overthrow Constantine.

To further show everyone they were different, the Christians got Constantine to establish Sunday as their day of rest and worship and that no judges would sit on the bench on Sunday.

No one was permitted to work on Sunday, so the Jews didn't work on Saturday or Sunday. The Christians thereby gained economically by this deal, because they started working on Saturday. Then new laws passed: Jews couldn't proselytize, Jews couldn't discourage other Jews from converting to Christianity, Jews couldn't intermarry with Christians or even "banquet" with them. Penalties for these offenses – death by burning. Then new laws – Jews couldn't own Christian slaves, then no slaves, then Jews were barred from military service, medicine, apothecaries. New synagogues couldn't be built. Old synagogues couldn't be repaired.

When Julian succeeded Constantine, he eventually restored most of the Jews' rights, but alas, he was only in power for two years. Later, the Theodosian Code of 458 C.E., reinstated all of Constantine's harsh laws. This Code became the basis for the codes of the Germanic kingdoms that replaced Roman rule in Western Europe.

However, Judaism was still recognized as a legal religion and was tolerated; but the hate was ingrained in the mind of others. With the rules of the game like they were, is it any wonder that the Christians gained dominance over everyone. First, you restrict and grind down your competitor who before being your competitor was your father. Then, you grind down the heathens and others who had not "heard of the word" by the sword. If they "accepted the word" they needn't fear the sword.

The Crusaders, of later times even, became the most ardent Zionists of all times. They had claimed that they had inherited the promise God made to the Children of Israel. They used this argument to induce thousands of followers to wrest the Holy Land from the Turks and restore it to themselves, the children of Israel. Zion again would belong to the New Israelites. Millions fought and were slaughtered over these crusades.

One reason Judaism didn't grow was its lack of proselytizing and its rigid stance to accepting converts unless they made all the overtures.

But that's ancient history, isn't it? Or is it really?

Chapter XXXIX

ARE THE JEWISH PEOPLE IMMORTAL?

BY MARK TWAIN, SEPTEMBER 1899

Probably, the Jew ought hardly to be heard of; but he is heard of. He is as prominent on this planet as any other people, and his commercial importance is extravagantly out of proportion to the smallness of his bulk. His contribution to the world's list of great names in literature, art, music, finance, medicine and abstruse learning are way out of proportion to the weakness of his numbers.

The Jew has made a marvelous fight in the world, in all ages, and has done it with his hands tied behind him. He could be vain of himself, and be excused for it.

The Egyptian, the Babylonian and the Persian, rose, filled the planet with sound and splendor, then faded to dream stuff and passed away; the Greek, the Roman followed, and made a vast noise, and they are gone. Other peoples have sprung up and held their torch high for a time, but it burned out and they sit in twilight now, or have vanished.

The Jew saw them all, beat them all, and is now what he always was, exhibiting no decadence, no infirmities of age, no weakening of his parts, no slowing of his energies, no dulling of his alert and aggressive mind. All things are mortal but the Jew; all other forces pass, but he remains. What is the secret of his immortality?

Samuel Clemens (Mark Twain) really had a favorable impression of Jews. He thought we were immortal. But he was not aware of indifference and assimilation. Here are our biggest battles. His daughter married a Jew.

Chapter XL
THE JEWS OF CHINA

Many of us have thrilled to the story of Marco Polo, whose trip to the Orient took many years, during which he encountered many hardships. We have read of his return with stories about gunpowder, incenses, silks, and other items "new" to Southern Europe and the Mediterranean. He is reported to be the first European to visit China. This is like saying that Columbus discovered America, which was full of Indians.

From around the 4th century B.C.E. to about the 2nd century C.E., the Judeans (Jews) had become the merchantmen of the known world. Together with Phoenician shipbuilders, the Jews financed the majority of the cargoes going to the known and "unknown" parts of the world. Large supercargoes were carried on Phoenician and Jewish ships. It is of interest to note that these ships carried all sorts of cargo, but very little gold. Jews, who had settled at the various ports where the trade routes touched, would write "notes" to other Jews for payment of cargo. These were accepted by other Jews, because the honor of both parties was at stake, sworn to on Torah, the law. Because of this practice, pirates learned that they wouldn't get gold by raiding Jewish ships. Consequently, ships flying Jewish flags were usually left alone.

The Jews established trade routes and settlements in India, Southern Asia and then China. The settlement in China is reputed to have been established around the year 67 C.E. The Chinese quickly accepted the Jews as men of honor. Why? They looked different than the Chinese, but many of their ways of living were the same. At that time Taoism was the religious practice of most Chinese – reverence for the elders being a strong feature. The Jews lived by a code – the Torah. Children obeyed their parents scrupulously. The word of a Jew, whether given to another Jew or a Chinese person, was upheld. Orthodox Jewry and Taoism bore many similarities. The Jew in a strange land believed in his honor (to keep face) and conducted himself in accordance with the laws of the Torah. These "People of the Book", as the Chinese called the Jews, impressed the Chinese very much.

Trade between the two peoples flourished. Jewish ships provided items of living that aided the Chinese, peasant and mandarin alike. In a time of famine, the Jews accepted the "word" of the Chinese and provided goods unstintingly. Later, the emperor of this area of China contributed to the building of a synagogue. When it burned down later, the emperor had a new one erected with Chinese labor according to the design of the Jews.

Jewish ships sent back silks, dye materials and spices to the Mediterranean and Persia. Trade routes were kept secret, if at all possible, to keep competition to a minimum. Persia was the hub of all the trade routes, because Persian Jews were involved in the first settlement in China at Kai Feng Fu. Most of the Jewish community had become assimilated by the 18th century. China is the only country in the world where the Jews experienced no anti-Semitism.

One of the Persian Jewish families who became large merchantmen and traders (even today) was the Sassoon family. A descendant of the Sassoon family lived in Sacramento after emigrating from Egypt (he was born in Brooklyn, NY, however). Today, there are estimated to be a handful (250–300) of Jews living in and around the Shanghai area. Hong Kong has a larger Jewish community.

Chapter XLI

THE JEWISH EMPIRE OF KHAZARIA

Did you know that from the 6th century to the 7th century an empire, sprawling from the lower Volta to the Northern Caucasus Mountains and beyond, was fashioned by conquering the Arabs, Magyars, Persians, Pechengs, West Turks, Rus, Ghuzz and other tribes? That this empire was a Jewish dominated empire, starting about 730 C.E.? That this empire was at times allied with Chinese, with West Turks, and with others?

The name "Khazaria" is mentioned in the histories, manuscripts, documents, letters, and such by many noted historians. That they were Jewish is also mentioned by many noted historians of a number of these nations. Where did they come from? Why Jews? Were they Semites? Where did they finally disappear? This is all difficult to unravel but people are still working on it.

The History of the Jewish Khazars by Professor D. M. Dunlop, Professor of Middle Eastern History at Columbia University, is the comprehensive authority on this subject. Indeed, this book is so full of references and bibliography (over 2,000 references) that it boggles your mind to figure out what was going on. I didn't know whether to read the bibliography material or the text, because it was a toss-up as to which contained more information. With no disrespect to the author, this book was one of the most difficult I have ever read, because of the author's need to justify each historical incident from more than one source. But on with our story.

According to some sources, when the Assyrian Empire broke up the land of Israel and deported ten of the twelve tribes to various places, the tribe of Simeon and half tribe of Manasseh were moved to the neighborhood of the Caucasus Mountains and the Caspian Sea. They brought their Torah with them and continued for a time as observant Jews, until with passing years the old timers passed on and less and less was remembered. The Torah and the other writings were hidden away in a cave to protect them from ravaging neighbors and there, more or less forgotten.

When the Muslims tried to extend their growing empire into Asia, they were stopped by fierce warriors known as Khazars (around 652 C.E.). The Khazars were protecting their own land from encroachment and were being assisted by a mysterious Khaqan-i-Chin (the Khaqan of China). Whether these helpers were Mongols or Chinese is not really known.

Also as part of legend (?) enter another origin of the Khazars. Hebrew owes some of its origin to the Ugarit language, not long ago unearthed in Syria. Well, the Uigurs existed both before and after the Turks. The *Tung-tien*, a Chinese work written in the period 766–801 C.E., mentions the Kosa (Khazars). A certain Tu Huan, who had become an Arab captive at the battle of Taraz in 751 C.E., returned to China in 762 C.E. Tu Huan referred to the Khazars as Kosa Turks, that they lived north of the Byzantine Empire, Khwarism and Persia. The Uigurs were composed of nine tribes the sixth of these being called the Kosa. According to one version of the *Tang-shu*, another Chinese work, the Uigurs are descended from the Huing-nu people (the Huns). But this is as early as 250 C.E. The Uigurs, apparently, themselves were Asiatic tribesmen who constantly moved west until they allied with the Bulgars and defeated the West Turks. Then they started to grow. Greek, Arabic, Chinese, Persian and other sources mention various events about the Khazars.

The Arabs tried to expand their empire and were beaten back. In time, the King (Khaqan) of the Khazars and his Beg (probably High Priest) ruled over people of many nations.

From their captives the Khazars learned about the Muslim and Christian religions. Both of these groups mentioned Judaism as their father religion but that they, of course, were the inheritors of the Word and the true Faith. Also, extant were stories of old books in a cave in their area preserved for many years and still used by people who practiced a form of Judaism.

Bhulan (the Khaqan), according to legend, sent for

representatives of the Jews and had debates carried on in his court. In 730 C.E. the king and his court reinstated Judaism, claiming it to be the religion of their ancestors and the one that stood the test of debate of learned men. The Khaqan permitted Muslims, Christians, Shamans and heathens, to live and coexist in his empire under Jewish rule. A number of the peoples took up Judaism because the Court did so, although most of the Generals were Muslims, and their influence on the Muslims in their armies was great.

Obadiah, the grandson of Bhulan, brought back many more Jewish rites and customs apparently from Jewish travelers and the Torah. They, by now, spoke a form of Hebrew and followed a Judaism that wasn't considered to be strictly according to the Torah.

At a later time, King Joseph of the Khazars is reported to have conducted correspondence with a MarHasday of the Spanish court, asking for news and in turn, giving many pieces of information about the Khazars. This was fictionalized later by Jehudah Halevi in his book *The Khazari*, in 1140 C.E.

During the Empire of the Khazars, however, they certainly conquered Kiev, the Crimea, the Caucasus, the Caspian Sea area and part of Armenia. The Rus tribe pushed them out of Kiev, or they withdrew by themselves. Certainly, Georgia, the Ukraine and Abkhazia were under their jurisdiction for periods, or at least, parts of these territories. Even a Russian Khaqan is mentioned in Arabic literature and Latin sources.

Around 913 C.E., the Russians who had consolidated a number of tribes, together attacked at a number of points along the Caspian shores and even got as far as Azerbaijan, but they withdrew. Later, in 943 C.E., they were again in the Caspian Sea and even built a fortification there. Apparently, the Khazars had let them in to fight the Muslim advances. Pestilence drove the Russians out, however. In 965 C.E., the Russians under their own Khaqan defeated the Khazars. The Khaqan's name was Sviatslav of the Kievan Russians. The capital of the Khazars (Atil) was laid waste. When the Khazars appealed to the Muslims for aid, they were told they couldn't help them because they were Jews, but if they became Muslims this maybe possible.

Twenty years later, the people of Khazaria returned, mostly Moslems, and took over. Most of the Russians had departed, and some sort of treaty was made to secure the area. The ruins of Atil became the town of Saqsin. It became a subservient state to the Russians and Saqsin became a large town on the Volga, the biggest in "Turkestan".

In the 13th century, hordes of Mongol invaders finally destroyed what was left of the Khazar state. However, the stories state that when Khazar was defeated in 965 C.E., the survivors organized under a Khaqan with Bosporus (Kertch) as their capital. Today, according to legend, many of the Crimean Jews are Khazarian descendants. Even the Karaites of that area are also thought to be Khazars. Who knows? There are so many theories, stories, documents that one's head swims. It seems safe to surmise that most of the Khazars became Muslims and then maybe Christian. Time may tell us the answers.

Chapter XLII
KHAZARIA REVISITED

Lately, there has been a rash of books, articles, etc., on new theories and counter theories regarding Khazaria. Let me bring you up to date. There is a book called *The Jews of Poland* by Bernard Weinryb (Jewish Publication Society), which states that most of the Jewish communities established around the globe owe their origin to the settlement by displaced Polish Jews. At one time, it was estimated that Poland had 10,000,000 Jews. This dispersion of Polish Jews is quite authenticated. But where did all the Polish Jews come from?

It was pretty well the consensus of scholars that Spain and other European localities supplied the original great influxes. The Roman Empire sent Jews to the Teutonic heartland of what is now Germany, Austria, and part of Poland as their merchants, emissaries, tradesmen, etc. The greatest numbers of these had settled around Cologne and Frankfurt and created Yiddish. That in itself is a long story, however, and digresses from the crux of this article. Now comes a new theory that the breakup of the Khazarian Empire caused large masses of Jews to travel to Poland and thereabouts. The Khazars stopped the invading Moslem (Arab) armies from invading Europe and Asia incidentally. The "Khs" stood between the Mongols and the Arabs and other tribal empires around the Black Sea, what is now Armenia, and the Caucasus.

Most of the writings about the "Khs" come from Arab chroniclers, who even reported that the "Khs" used the Hebrew script in writing. Muqassi (10th century), Ibn Nadim (10th century), Al-Bakri (11th century), all wrote about the "Khs". So if the new theory is true, most of the Jews today are related not to ancestors from the land of Palestine or the pre-Inquisition Spanish Empire, but from the Huns, Uigurs and Magyars of the

Caucasus region. Khazaria was at the height of its power from the seventh to the tenth centuries and was finally overcome by the Rus Empire, believed to be descendants of the Vikings and the origin of the name "Russia". In fact, the Caspian Sea was called the "Sea of the Khazars". Even today, Odessa in the Crimea is twenty-five per cent Jewish in population. Stalin came from Georgia, located in this area, as is Azerbaijan.

So if what Arthur Koestler, the author of *The Thirteenth Tribe* says is true, we Jews are indeed a mixed bag of peoples, closer to Oriental than to other groups of peoples. To get back to the 7th century and later, the Khazars prevented the Byzantine Empire from expanding.

One thing different about the Khazarian Empire; within its borders they permitted the practice of any or no religion. In fact, to insure this, their Supreme Court consisted of two Jews, two Christians, two Moslems and one pagan. The people were farmers, cattle breeders, fishermen, tradesmen, wine makers and artisans until the call to arms, when they became warriors again. Two hundred years after their supposed defeat by the Rus tribes or Vikings, they reportedly still had a standing army. What really caused the empire to collapse is the onslaught of Genghis Khan. You must read Koestler's book *The Thirteenth Tribe: The Khazar Empire and its Heritage* (Random House Publishers).

Chapter XLIII

THE JEWISH REFUGEES OF MIDDLE EAST: A SURVEY

BY DR. EDMOND ROTH, TEL AVIV

Before 1948, 1,100,000 Jews lived in the Arab countries, including North Africa. The persecuted Jews of these countries had no other choice but to immigrate to Israel and spend a period of four to five years living in refugee slums, tents and tin shacks. But, as compared with less than 500,000 Arabs who left Israel at the express instruction of the Supreme (Moslem) Council of the Mufti of Jerusalem and failed to receive their rights in the countries that absorbed them, the Jewish refugees in Israel immediately obtained full civil rights and made their way up the social, socio-cultural and economic ladder.

According to statistics gathered by Professor Yehezkel Hadar – a Jew of Iraqi origin who lives in New York, 794,000 Middle East Jews arrived in Israel up to 1962, according to the following breakdown:

Algeria	110,000
Egypt	90,000
Iraq	125,000
Lebanon	1,000
Libya	33,000
Morocco	250,000
Syria	35,000
Tunisia	75,000
Yemen, Aden	75,000

Since 1960, another 30,000 Jews from Arab states reached Israel. Taking the Arabs' own method of calculating the number of (their) refugees, including their offspring, there are now in Israel more than 1,400,000 Jews from Arab countries.

In 1962, when the first independent government of Algeria expelled 140,000 Jews and took over all their immovable property within a number of weeks, the Israel government issued no public protest. The same phenomenon occurred in 1966, when the 5,000 strong Jewish community of Aden was uprooted from where it had lived continuously for almost 3,000 years.

In 1952, when Dr. Edmond Roth verified statistics on the property of the Jewry of Tunisia, Morocco, and Tangier, he found that the value of the real estate property held by Jews in those countries then totaled about three billion dollars. It is also worth noting that Jewish geologists and administrators were very active in the discovery and development of the Algerian oil fields. On the basis of his examinations, he assessed the stolen property of Arab Jewry, including real estate properties, movable belongings, money, and businesses at seven billion dollars, according to 1962 prices.

Israel and the Arab states have effectively carried out an exchange of populations, since 1948, and the numerical balance favors the Arab states. In at least two cases, this exchange has been ratified "de jure" by Arab governments such as Yemen and Iraq.

The world should also be reminded that two World Wars allowed for the establishment of twenty Arab states on territory of about twelve million square kilometers. About 70,000 Jewish soldiers and officers served in the allied armies in the first war and 600,000 in the second. It was not Sadat, then sitting in a British jail for spying on behalf of the Nazis, who saved Egypt from the Nazi German takeover, but rather, the British army in which Jewish officers and men served.

Chapter XLIV
SPAIN

Much has been written on the Spanish Inquisition and its effect on Jewry, the Moors, Spain and the Catholic Church of that era! The following information has been excerpted from a paper by Dr. Wayne Grossman and has, of necessity, been shortened to fit herein. Just to lay a little bit of the groundwork for a more thorough understanding of the situation, some geography and economics are included right here about the Iberian Peninsula.

The Iberian Peninsula was divided into four monarchies – Portugal, Castile, Granada and Aragon. Castile contained two-thirds of the Peninsula and three-quarters of the population and greater wealth than Portugal and Aragon together. The Moors still held the kingdom of Granada (Southern Spain), while the other monarchies were Catholic. Castile still was trying to dislodge the hold of the Moors in Granada – who had held it from the 8th century. Castile wanted Granada not to get rid of the Moslems, but to get the land. For hundreds of years the Christians, Jews, and Moors, had lived in each of the kingdoms side by side, separate, yet tolerant of each other. These peoples shared a common culture, which overshadowed their religious beliefs.

In 1212, the Moors were defeated at Las Navas de Tolosa by advancing Christians who then started to act like conquerors. Why then, when for years they had all lived side by side? Except for two exceptions there had been no real religious oppression until the 14th century. These exceptions were the massacre of 4,000 Jews by the Moors in Granada, on December 30, 1066 and in 1250 (approximately), the widespread killing of both Jews and Christians by Almoravid Moors. These particular Moors forced conversion on a large number of Jews and Christians. But by 1212, the Christians felt strong enough to overcome the status quo that existed in Spain.

What was the status quo? The Christian population made war and tilled the soil, the Moors built houses, and the Jews acted as fiscal agents (financiers) and skilled technicians (doctors, silversmiths, dyers, cloth weavers, etc.). However, about one and a half per cent of the population owned ninety-seven per cent of the land – the Christian Nobles and the Church hierarchy. They made, literally, millions of dollars in income per year and in Castile even the Crown made an alliance with the Nobles. And now, on to the paper.

Chapter XLV

THE EFFECT OF THE EXPULSION OF THE JEWS AND MOORS ON THE DECLINE OF SPAIN

BY DR. WAYNE GROSSMAN

Part I

The Jewish people have been persecuted since time immemorial. In Moorish Spain, however, the Jews lived in relative peace and tranquility. The Jews thrived upon the knowledge that was made available to them through Mohammedan scholars. In this land, unlike most of Europe, the Jews were not restricted to the "degrading" occupation of money lending. The Jews were able to develop their talents in medicine, science, professions, crafts and arts. They flourished as they had in no other nation in Europe. Even as Christianity swallowed up the country, the Jews enjoyed what has come to be known as the Golden Age of Judaism.

The historian Americo Castro speaks of the Jews of Castile, "their Jewish subjects... have been the most distinguished Jews that there have been in all the realms of the dispersion; they are distinguished in four ways: in lineage, in wealth, in virtues, in science." The Jews, some of whom had lived in Spain since the 1st century C.E. constituted so important and so influential a minority that, after a few initial massacres out of sheer habit, the Christians thought it advisable to leave them undisturbed in the newly conquered Moorish territories for fear that the Jews would unite militarily with the Moors.

Once the Moorish menace was ended, however, the necessity for conciliating the Jewish minority diminished. Their position began to deteriorate as anti-Jewish legislation and other restrictions made their appearance. In 1391, events took a tragic step. Fired up by fanatical leaders like Martinez, frenzied mobs attacked Jewish communities all over Spain. The mobs murdered, looted, pillaged, and burned while the authorities made but a few feeble efforts to control them. Entire Jewish communities such as those of Cordova and Toledo were exterminated as over seventy communities throughout Spain were attacked. Onslaughts on the Jews became the order of the day. All over Spain, Jews yielded to baptism in order to save their lives. The forced converts, or conversos, formed ever-increasing ranks. Although outwardly professing Christianity, many of these conversos secretly remained loyal Jews. They would take their children for baptism at birth but would in secret teach them the Jewish faith. The conversos formed a tightly-knit community that kept many ties with the Jewish community. When it became apparent that these new Christians were not loyal to their adopted religion, the Inquisition was established by a Papal Bull in 1478.

The Spanish Inquisition, then, was established primarily to take care of the problem of the conversos who secretly practiced Judaism, the Marranos. The Marranos had come to be feared more than the Jews for they were considered to be a fifth column within the body of the Church. With the advent of the Inquisition, Spain became a police state where people feared that they would be denounced for even a minor action that might be construed as the action of a Jew or Converso. When a suspect was arrested, all of his property and goods were quickly seized. Even if the suspect was later found to be innocent, his property still belonged to the church or State.

Part II

Historians give various reasons why the Jews were banished from Spain. Castro states that, "the people would no longer tolerate the pre-eminent position of the Hispano-Hebrews now that Spain had conquered the last remaining Moors in the Peninsula". The Jews felt proud of belonging to a powerful nation, whose very strength and efficiency, by the way, owed much to the Jews. The Christian populace was irritated by the economic and technical superiority of its Semitic compatriots. The Christians wanted the Jews to get out, regardless of the consequences. They did this while knowing fully well that there would be no one to take care of many of the essential tasks that for centuries had been the occupations of the Jews. Hugh Trevor-Roper puts forth the view, in *"Limpieza"*, that: "the Inquisition and expulsion was primarily the product of the hatred and rivalry of the lower classes and their clergy, although both actions may have been initiated by nobility." Henry Kamen takes a somewhat opposite view when he states that: "The expulsion of the Jews was more than a religion move; in its widest interpretation, it was also an attempt by the nobility to eliminate that section of the middle classes, the Jews, which was threatening its ascendancy in the state. It was a refusal by the old order to accept the increasing importance of those who were in control of the capital and the commerce of the towns."

Bertrand and Petrie, in *The History of Spain,* propose yet another reason for the expulsion. They note that it was only after the taking of this last citadel of Islam in Spain (Granada), that the general expulsion of the Jews was decreed. What was specially (sic) feared was the alliance of the Jews with the Granadan Moors who remained in Spain. Perhaps the reason for the expulsion was a product of these various arguments. Whatever the case, as Trevor-Roper points out, "In one hundred and thirty years the Inquisition had gone far beyond the correction of heresy: it had 'purified' the race and incidentally, simplified the class structure of Spain. The decreasing number of Marrano trials at the tribunals of the Spanish Inquisition during the seventeenth and eighteenth centuries, indicates that marranism died out gradually and virtually disappeared in Spain itself, a century before the Inquisition tribunals were abolished early in the 19th century.

The first objective of the Inquisition after the secret Jews was the secret Moors. The Moors, of course, had been numerous in Spain since their incursion in 711 A.D. In the early years of the Christian re-conquest, the Mohammedans were butchered in every conquered town until a more conciliatory policy developed as the Christians realized that their defenseless co-religionists of the southern peninsula were left open to reprisals. To facilitate the re-conquest, surrendering Muslim communities in most areas were guaranteed religious liberty through treaties. So, by the second half of the 14th century, most of Spain was in the hands of the Christian princes and from this point, the re-conquest continued slowly. The last Moorish stronghold to fall was Granada. The Moors were very strong when they surrendered Granada after the ten-year war for it. Because they were still so powerful, the Spanish granted them unthinkable concessions in order to end the war. The treaty that was signed amounted in effect to recognition of a "Moorish nation" maintained in a privileged position within Spanish territory. The question has been raised as to why the Moors weren't quickly eliminated or driven out after the Christian conquest of Granada. Bertrand and Petrie feel that it was because the Christians didn't want to ruin the commerce and agriculture of their new territories. Besides, it was a long-standing custom among the Christian princes to prefer protectorate with payment of tribute, to complete conquest and expulsion or extermination. They thus created tributaries, which cost nothing and paid handsomely. The Christian princes, then, simply took the conquered enemy's money and sold him the right to live and own property. Since this system worked so well it is little wonder that the re-conquest continued only slowly.

The Spanish monarchs found it increasingly difficult to keep the pledges to the Moorish communities under the pressures of the Christian religious zealots. The official policy soon became one of inducement to leave by an underhanded system of oppression and of pressure aimed to bring them to baptism. As the pressure was backed up by force, the Moors rebelled. After a succession of unsuccessful revolts, the Moors of Castile and Granada were offered either expulsion or baptism. There was really little choice in the matter for such engrossing restrictions were made to keep them from emigrating. Here were formed the large number of secret Moors, or Moriscos (Moslems who converted under duress), with which the Inquisition also concerned itself. In 1525, Charles V proclaimed that no Mohammedan shall remain in all his kingdom, thus putting fact into law. The Moriscos still formed a close-knit community, which was not able to be brought completely into the Church. They were overtaxed and looked down upon the rest of the population. Finally, the Moriscos felt that they had nothing to lose and revolted again in December 1568. After a hard-fought war of two years, the Moriscos were beaten. The Granadans were deported en masse and scattered throughout Spain. The final order of expulsion of all the Moriscos came in 1609. By 1614, an estimated one million Moriscos had left Spain.

Historians generally regard the expulsion of the Moors and Moriscos with less condemnation than they view the expulsion of the Jews. Bertrand and Petrie very strongly hold the view that the Christians had justification, though not necessarily religious, for expelling the Moslems. They hold that the Moors were true enemies of Spain. The Moslems spoke a different language, had a different religion, had ties with enemies of Spain in Africa, and despised the Christians. Spain, they feel, was justified in doing whatever necessary to remove the Moorish menace.

By attacking and expelling the Jews and Marranos, the government destroyed the middle class of Spain of which the Jews had comprised a major part. There is little debate over whether the Jews did comprise this segment of the population, for this goes nearly undisputed. The argument is over the importance of this group to the overall well-being of Spain. One of the ties of the middle class, in particular the Jewish middle class, is to capitalism. Capitalism was just developing in Spain at about the time of the expulsions. There is little question that it was retarded, for Spain has never really developed a strong capitalistic system. Some support for this view of finance was soon filled not by Spaniards but by foreigners, particularly Genoese and Germans. This situation changed somewhat later on, in the 17th century, when converso financiers fleeing from the Portuguese Inquisition were allowed to remain in Spain. A conciliatory attitude developed among Spanish leaders, for the Jewish finances were welcomed. The Portuguese conversos soon held leading positions as bankers of the Crown but a reaction set in which saw the persecution and condemnation of many of these financiers. "Here, in the direct confrontation between the Inquisition and men of finance, lies the opportunity to prove that the tribunal destroyed the intelligent creation and manipulation of capital and so retarded industry and destroyed investment in Spain" (Kamen). Olive Day, in *A History of Commerce*, also sees this disastrous confrontation between progressive interests and ecclesiastical power that so came to dominate Spain in this atmosphere of illogic.

Men of business sense were excluded from office even in the towns, as far as possible, and were a rarity in the national parliament; power lay in the hands of lay and ecclesiastical lords who had inherited feudal ideas, the reverse of businesslike ideas, from the earlier period of the crusade against the Moors, and who had no understanding of the measures needed for industrial development.

This period of Spanish history then saw a disregard for the importance of capitalism and industrial development. The most advanced classes in manufactures and trade were not the native Christians but Moors or Jews. In eliminating these classes, Spain condemned herself to a menial place in the business world of Europe. With the tremendous riches that poured in from her colonies, Spain could have established her place at the top in the commerce of Europe had she not so foolishly destroyed the skillful manipulators of wealth within her realm. The Jews had not only controlled the capitalistic element of finance, thus paying a large percentage of the tax monies, but they were also the principal tax collectors for the princes and the Crown. For centuries, this job had fallen on the heads of the Jews and now it was difficult to find others to take their place. In one way or another, the income of the treasury proceeded from Jews or had of necessity to pass through their hands. Here lies another reason for the decline of Spanish power.

Not only did the loss of the Jews have an effect on the economy of Spain, but also the loss of the Moors and Moriscos further impoverished the country. It must be noted that the Moorish elements of Spain numbered perhaps one million out of a total population of about seven million. The Moors clearly had an important influence in commerce, for they were very active in trade and even small manufacturing. What was much more significant, though, was the agricultural importance of the Moors. They composed perhaps the largest and most highly skilled element of the agricultural class. It is further necessary to consider the overall population loss of Spain, stemming from the expulsions. Historians regard this sudden loss of about one-seventh of the population of Spain as a major cause of the nation's decline.

When the Moriscos left, there were few in Spain who could take their place in the fields. During the 17th century, people had to be brought from other countries, in particular from France, to do the reaping and some of the others, harvesting. Because of the loss of the Moors and Jews, a large portion of the labor and craftsmen needed in Spain had to be imported as well. What was the native Christian population doing as the cultivated land was laid waste and left barren and commerce and industry was floundering? It seems that they became so caught up in the doctrines of the Inquisition that, by the late 18th century, nearly one-third of the total adult male population of the peninsula had evolved into the clergy and other privileged classes. Not only did these classes not work, but they also did not pay direct and even some indirect taxes. Spain has never fully recovered from this period of its history, neither agriculturally nor commercially.

It must be remembered that the princes and monarchs of Spain had developed a system of tribute in regard to the Moriscos. The Moriscos paid heavy taxes in order to protect their lives and keep their property from being confiscated. In some areas, the revenue of tribunals consisted of over forty percent of money taken from the Moriscos. The Moriscos in the realms of Aragon were supporting a tribunal, which was devoted to the destruction of their religion and culture. Once the expulsions came, this system, of course, collapsed. In Saragosa, for example, the tribunal income of the year before the expulsion amounted to 61,615 reales and after the expulsion to 32,175 reales. Once the expulsions were instituted, the tribunals and the nobility lost a great percentage of their incomes, further weakening the economic structure of Spain.

When the Spaniards expelled the Jewish and Moorish elements of their population, they took an incalculable loss in terms of further cultural development. The Jews and Moors were not only the leaders in commerce, agriculture and the crafts, but they also had held the leading positions as educators, scientists, physicians and writers. The greatness of these people is to a degree indicated by the names of some of those who were descended from Marrano stock who had eventually found refuge in other nations: Benjamin Disraeli, Prime Minister of England; Benedict Spinoza, father of modern philosophy; David Ricardo, founder of the school of political economics; Sir Arthur Wing Pinero, one of the great figures in modern English drama. Spain, however, obsessed with the goal of purifying the race, chose to sacrifice intellectual superiority for a menial position among the nations of the world.

Chapter XLVI

URIAH P. LEVY

BY HAL SCHACHTER

Uriah P. Levy, famed naval hero, served his country with great distinction from the war of 1812 to his final year 1862. Through sheer hard work and brilliance, he climbed from sailing master to Commodore, then the Navy's highest rank, the equal today of rising from chief petty officer to Admiral.

Levy was one of the first naval officers to recognize men for their ability, and not classing them by ethnic roots or social standing. When commander of the USS Vandalia during the War of 1812, he fathered a law that would secure his name in history, the law that abolished flogging in the Navy. This fact is inscribed on his tombstone in Cypress Hills Cemetery, New York City.

Before the Naval Academy came into existence, Commodore Levy wrote and published the *Manual of Rules for Men of War*, the first printed guide book for young officers' duties aboard ship, a work that ran into three editions, up to and including the "new age of steam".

A devoted admirer of Thomas Jefferson, Levy, on a visit to Paris, paid his respects to the aging Lafayette who was saddened to hear the great Jefferson had died penniless and wondered what had happened to beautiful Monticello. Levy didn't know. But not for long. He found the mansion and grounds suffering from years of neglect and decay. He purchased Monticello on May 20, 1836 and labored to restore and preserve it for unborn generations.

Uriah Levy was a religious man, belonging to two synagogues. He was the first president of the Washington Hebrew Congregation, and a member of Shearith Israel Congregation in New York (the oldest existing in the US today).

In World War II, the destroyer USS Levy was named in his

memory. Thus, it was only natural that the first permanent Jewish Chapel ever to be built by the US armed forces should also honor his memory. You are warmly invited to visit the Commodore Levy Chapel near the main gate of the historic Naval Station in Norfolk, VA.

Chapter XLVII
THE "RUSSIAN" JEWS

In the 8th century B.C.E., the Assyrians conquered Israel and decided to disperse the people as much as possible. They conducted Jews to Médéa, Persia, and to the Bosporus. In the 6th century B.C.E., Babylonia conquered Judea and another group headed for the same area, the Bosporus. In the 1st century C.E., the Romans conquered Jerusalem and moved a group of Jews to the Bosporus area. More Jews headed to the land between the Black Sea and the Caspian Sea as time went on. In the 9th century C.E., Vikings from Sweden came down the rivers from the Baltic Sea to Kiev. The Vikings were known as the "Rus" or "Rowers". Jews were there to greet them.

Nothing much of historical importance occurred until 1500. Two Jews who had been forcibly converted to Christianity began to preach Judaism to the Russian peasants, resulting in many conversions to Judaism. The Russian Orthodox Church believed this was heresy and made death the punishment for those who converted. In addition, the Jews were expelled. In the 17th century, Russia annexed parts of Lithuania and received more Jews than those who were expelled. Russia, then, kicked the Jews out again. But Russia, under Peter the Great, took the Baltic countries – which contained many Jews – from Sweden. From 1725 to 1762, the Jews were considered as foreigners. Moslems were also persecuted vigorously.

In the 1760s, Catherine the Great granted religious liberty to all subjects in Russia, including Jews. In 1772, Russia conquered part of Poland. She got more of Poland in 1793 and 1795. This brought in 900,000 more Jews under Russian rule, most of them illiterate. Catherine then permitted these Polish Jews to live in an area from Riga to Rostov on the Sea of Azov. This area became known as the "Pale of Settlement". There were certain areas there where Jews were not allowed to live except by special permission – Kiev, Yalta, Sevastopol.

After another century, there were 300,000 Russian Jews, highly intellectual, well-to-do and rather elite in Russian cities; 1,700,000 proletarian Jews living in Russian held Poland; and 3,000,000 Jews in the Pale of Settlement. In the Pale, the Jews lived a degraded existence. Here, the Torah and Talmud were not studied as a rule and an oral law took shape. The Jews made obsessive rituals and laws upon laws that they attributed to Moses and God – laws and rituals not covered by the Torah or the Talmud. Trivia and absurdity was commonplace and these laws were added to the Talmud and taught to the children. These teachers (Talmudists) hated the Chasidim and denounced them to the Russian police. The Chasidim had to be protected from Talmudists and fanatic Christians under three czars, Catherine the Great, Paul I and Alexander I.

The Russians wanted to introduce a modern school system in the Pale, but the Jews kept their cheders (schools) and did not want any secular education to reach their children. In the 1800s, when a czar started a liberal policy to all the people, the nobility opposed it. When a restrictive policy was enacted, a people's rebellion brewed. The Romanov czars were weak and inept. Alexander I enacted a policy of very little restrictions and much liberty towards the Jews. The Orthodox Jews did not want to give up their autonomy, for they thought that a secular education would loosen the bonds on their children. Alexander I wanted to encourage agricultural training for the Jews, get them a secular education and permit the Jews in the Pale to live everywhere. He wanted to "Westernize" his Jews, but the orthodoxy put up fierce resistance. He wanted his Jews to go into law, medicine, math and science, also. But no, the Jews in the Pale did not go along. However, the Jews in Russia proper (Moscow, St. Petersburg. Minsk, Odessa) fought to get into schools of higher education. In 1879, the czars abandoned their plan to educate the Jews of the Pale.

In Lithuania, a Talmudist (not from the Pale of Settlement) criticized the Orthodox Jews of the Pale and called them ignoramuses. He excommunicated them even though he was not a rabbi. He was the Vilna Gaon (1720–1797). He encouraged his students to study science and to reject the trivial teachings of these Ultra Orthodox.

In Israel today, we see some of the same philosophy of the Orthodox Jews of the Pale. If you do not believe the way that they do, you are an outsider and a threat. Our history is not always one of progress, clear thinking and enlightenment.

Chapter XLVIII

THE NEGEV DESERT

The southern part of Israel is a desolate, arid region with resultant salt formations, untillable land and brackish water where surface water has been found. Israel is a very small country, which hopes to take in millions of Jews. But where to put them? If the desert can be transformed into a hospitable place, that would be a possible solution.

Nearby this desert, in Be'er Sheva', is the Ben-Gurion University (BGU). To the scientists and scholars there, this desert is a challenge. The results of taking this challenge may indeed change the world's future. Here are some of the accomplishments of these BGU personnel:

Professor Arie Issar proved that there was a literal ocean of water that was trapped after the last Ice Age in a large underground aquifer. But this water was high in salts and gypsum. BGU scientists, however, grew crops with this water – wheat, tomatoes, cucumbers and even watermelons. So, wastelands can be reclaimed all over the world using brackish water where no fresh water is available. The pumping of water from the aquifer will boost the economy of this desert by developing agriculture.

Fruit and nut trees that now grow wild in the desert are being domesticated to grow with little water. They developed a technique for growing almond and pistachio trees on as little as two cups of water per year. BGU people have done other things also, like working to make camels the dairy cows of the desert. Camel milk is highly nutritious and does not turn sour, according to reports.

Pond scum, or micro algae, is another development that can be a source of pigments for use in markers in medical diagnostics, food coloring and cosmetics. Professor Arnon Shani has been leading this work. This alga also has the potential to biologically treat industrial wastewater.

Dr. Esther Priel found that an overlooked cancer drug was effective in stopping development of an enzyme that affects the AIDS virus. Professor Joel Margaith found and developed an unknown strain of bacteria that kills larvae of a tropical blackfly whose bite annually blinds more than 70,000 people in Africa.

But, in spite of all the above, BGU has a problem – lack of money. If there were more money to work on various other projects that could help all nations, this would be a boon to mankind. If you care to help, the American Associates of BGU will gladly accept your contribution. You could be instrumental in supporting the development of a new energy source or natural chemicals to control insect vermin or new vegetable strains or microbial control of plant diseases.

American Associates of Ben-Gurion University
342 Madison Avenue
Suite 1224
New York 10173

Chapter XLIX

THE GOLAN HEIGHTS PROBLEM

Since when is an attacker granted land that he lost to the "attacked"? Did the US give Texas back to Mexico? Or California to Mexico? Did Japan give back the land they took after the Russo-Japanese War? Did anyone in history return land to the beaten country? No. But Israel is being asked to, by the US, Russia and other countries to do just that. And the Arab countries, naturally.

The Golan and Jordan were part of Palestine for years and years. After World War I in 1923, France with the consent of Britain gave the Golan to Syria. And Britain gave the eastern part of Palestine to a member of the Hashemite family – Jordan. The Golan was the home of the Manasseh tribe after the Jews returned from Egypt under Joshua. Jews lived there for a couple of thousand years. In 1917, Britain noted that the Golan was Jewish territory.

Under the Syrians the Golan was mostly barren. Now there are 17,000 Jews in one city and thirty more villages. There are small factories, a winery, Israel's largest dairy farm and electricity generated by windmills. There are also 13,000 Druze. One-third of Israel's water supply originates in the Golan.

It is believed by military experts that giving the Golan to Syria is a step towards suicide. And if the US has to send men to monitor the area as part of UN force, that step is detested by the US citizen. Little by little Israel is losing land, protection and security by peace attempts. What it gained during wars it is losing by politics.

Chapter L

WORLD WAR II JEWISH RECORDS

I met many anti-Semites when I was in the Navy in World War II. They would tell me that Jews did not serve, they bought their way out of service. Also, some thought we had horns. But the Bureau of War records published facts regarding service by Jews.

In World War II, half a million Jews served. The percentage of Jews in uniform was higher than that of the general population. 1,157 died in service; over 35,000 were casualties (22,000 in combat), 15,000 received citations for valor and merit; our men (and women) received over 29,000 awards. Only one received the Congressional Medal of Honor, and sixty-seven the Distinguished Service Cross or Navy Cross. Fifteen were Generals, three were Admiral or Commodore. One third of all Jewish doctors were in uniform.

Thousands of Jewish families had three or more members in service: thirteen families had six; twelve families had seven and three families had eight. I come from a family with eight brothers in the service; another brother worked on parts of the atomic bomb (unknown to him at that time); and another was a peace officer (a constable) in Pittsburgh. I was youngest of ten brothers.

Chapter LI

ONE MAN'S OPINION – EPILOGUE

Too many of us who are born Jews do not know as much about Judaism as ninety per cent of those who are converts to Judaism. And just why is that so? Isn't that a rather startling statistic to "dump into your lap"? Well, let me show you why I sincerely believe this.

Most of us who are Jewish by birth just grow into the things that are Jewish. We see our mother light shabbos candles – if yours did – when we were little. Later, we may see our Dad go to Shul or Temple. We hear about this holiday, and that holiday, a little at a time. We get it piece meal, history mixed in with custom, mixed in with "bobbameisas" (old wives tales), mixed in with opinions. Then we hear about the same holidays from someone else, except that what we hear is different.

As we get older, we attend Services. No one taught you in advance the songs, the words, the prayers, the why of certain rituals. You were just told to do them, or you listened or you did them because you would be embarrassed not to. Perhaps you went to Sunday School or Cheder. In Sunday school, you get more information about the Festivals and about the Torah and some Jewish history. Many times, because you get a piece of information here and piece there, it doesn't all tie together like a neat package or like a story with a beginning, middle, and an end.

So, the "kids" grow up just waiting to get it over with. What they have been fed in once or twice a week "meals", they don't relate to very well. Then someone passes away among your relatives and you see another group of customs come into play. Except that most adults do not even know what is the proper thing to do for the specific occasion. And if your folks were orthodox and the people who died were reform or vice versa, you have different customs, etc., ad infinitum.

Those who convert to Judaism have to read suggested books and other matter to know what they are "getting", to learn about what Jews believe in, to know why we do certain things, etc. And in a rather orderly fashion, I believe. Because the convert has had a close look at Judaism, its philosophy, and continuity, he really has a strong feeling of wanting to be a part of something that is beautiful. Many of us born as Jews, either take it for granted, or have a "so what?" feeling about it.

Why? I say it because these same Jews do not know what Judaism is really all about! Many of us do not do any or enough reading. Well, it's time we learned! We should stop being ignorant! Yes, we may be intelligent (some of us), but we're still ignorant of facts that we should know. I'd like to make a recommendation to all of you reading this article. I'd also like to make a recommendation to our Sunday Schools.

There is a pocket book that I personally feel will help bridge this gap. It's easy to read, has about 179 pages, and answers all sorts of questions you might have wondered about but didn't ask. It is called: *What is a Jew?* by Rabbi Morris N. Kertzer. The Sunday Schools should require that the students read this book at as early an age as possible. At any rate, it should be read before Bar Mitzvah or Confirmation time. Then, if you think it wise, you could hold discussions with the students in class or "debate it" if you wish. You adults out there buy some bestsellers or a book of the month or sexy magazines at the drop of a hat. Go out and buy this book NOW! I'm not sure, but maybe the Judaica Shop or Sisterhood Stores in the synagogues have this in hand.

I welcome rebuttal to anything I've said here. Incidentally, this book is just the thing for any of your Gentile friends to read who wish to learn about Judaism. But you should read it before they do so that you won't be embarrassed when they ask you questions that you can't answer.

Chapter LII
A GUIDE FOR THE BEREAVED

Although modern Jewish practice is open to many options, we are often questioned as to proper procedures, during the period of mourning. I hope that special notice will be paid to those that are capitalized, as in contemporary Judaism; the individual mourner should feel free to be guided by his own sense of propriety and dignity. For those, who want a guide, these are some recommended procedures:

Mourning

1. Mourning is required for father, son, daughter, brother, sister, husband and wife, as well as step-parents and stepchildren – also for foster parents and adopted children, even if any of them are non-Jewish.
2. It is not required to mourn for children less than eight days old.
3. The first phase of mourning begins with the moment of death and ends with the burial of the deceased. During this period of grief, the bereaved should engage in no other matter than those pertaining to the funeral, except in emergencies.
4. The second phase of mourning begins with the day of the burial and lasts for three days. During these first three days, which include the funeral, the mourner should refrain from work and remain at home. This applies especially to the first day, even if the mourner works for others. On the other two days, he may attend to his occupation if it involves considerable loss – also, children may attend school.
5. A physician or nurse may attend to the seriously ill even on the first day of mourning, but should contribute the proceeds of that day to religious or charitable causes in memory of the

deceased.

6. During this three-day period the mourner should devote time to the study of the Torah in memory of his beloved deceased. His friends and visitors should not engage in idle talk. Nor should they do more than taste the food and drink in the mourner's house. (A house of mourning ought not become a house of feasting and mirth.)

7. Minyan Service: A service the evening of the funeral and the first morning after is usually sufficient – although one may have these services for a week. These services were instituted for those accustomed to daily worship and to whom the laws of mourning forbid going to the synagogue, except on the Sabbath, during the seven-day mourning period.

8. Women should attend these services. The number ten, (a minyan) although desirable, is not required to hold them – any number can hold them. It is perfectly permissible for laymen to conduct these services.

9. During the three-day period of mourning, the Yahrtseit light should be lit and remain lit as a memorial to the deceased.

10. During the three-day period of mourning, the mourner should make no effort to seek entertainment, public or private.

11. There are many who extend the three days to seven days. (Shivah)

12. The third phase of mourning continues for a period of one year. During the first thirty days, including the three-day period of bereavement, the mourner should not attend any public entertainments.

13. During this month, exclusive of the first three days of mourning, a mourner may attend congregational affairs as well as civic and philanthropic meetings.

14. A mourner may attend circumcision of his son even during the first three days of mourning and also the wedding service of an immediate relative. Following the first month, the mourner may resume his normal social life in accordance with his readiness to do so.

15. Remarriage should not occur until at least ninety days have passed.

Chapter LIII

KADDISH AND YAHRTSEIT

1. Kaddish should be recited by the mourners for all members of the immediate family on the day of the funeral and a year thereafter, once a week on the Sabbath.
2. Graves of the deceased members of the family should not be visited during the first week after burial nor on the Sabbath, festivals, or holidays.
3. Upon visiting the city where one's parents or other members of the immediate family are buried, one should not leave without visiting their graves and reciting a prayer there.
4. Monuments on graves should be placed during the first year following death, but not before the first month after burial. The prevailing custom has usually been 11 months. There need be no unveiling ceremony unless the family desires.
5. Yahrtseit, anniversary of the death of a loved one, should begin with the evening preceding the date of death. It should be observed annually throughout the lifetime of surviving members of the immediate family by kindling the Yahrtseit light at home.
6. The light should remain lit in the house from sundown to sundown on the anniversary of his/her death.
7. Yahrtseit may be observed by attending Sabbath worship services on the Sabbath approximate to that date.

BIBLIOGRAPHY

Professor Chomski, *Origin of Hebrew*, Jewish Publication Society, 1967

Yehezkah Kaufmann, *Great Hopes and Ideas of the Jewish People*, Part I, 1956

F. M. Schweitzer, A. *History of the Jews Since the First Century A.D.*, Anti-defamation League of B'nai B'rith, 1971 (Author is Roman Catholic and Member of History Department of Manhattan)

Max I. Dimont, *Jews, God and History*, Simon and Schuster, 1962

Kevin Starr, California historian remarks, 1976

Near East Report

Dr. Edmond Roth, Tel Aviv Settlement Specialist, 1975

Ha'aretz, Israeli newspaper, 1976

American Airlines, 1977–78

Stephen Birmingham, *Great Jewish Families of New York*, 1967

Encyclopedia Britannica

World Book Encyclopedia

Howard Fast, *The Jews – Story of A People*, 1968

Gratz, *History of the Jews*

Encyclopedia Americana

H. J. Levine and B. Miller, "The American Jewish Farmer", *Changing Times*, 1966

Jewish Agricultural Society

Martin Lowenthal, *The Diaries of Theodor Herzl*, Grosset & Dunlop, 1962

The *Talmud,* 400 B.C.E. to 1200 C.E.

Louis Bertrand and Sir Charles Petrie, *The History of Spain*, Macmillan, 1952

Americo Castro, *The Structure of Spanish History*, Editorial Porrua, Mexico, 1954

Clive Day, *A History of Commerce*, Longmans, Green & Co., 1940

Henry Kamen, *Confiscations in the Economy of the Spanish Inquisition*, New American Library, 1966

Henry Kamen, *Decline of Castille: The Last Crises,* New America Library, 1966

Henry Kamen, *Spanish Inquisition*, New America Library, 1966

Harcourt, *Violent Past*, James Morris, Brace & World, 1964

Cecil Roth, *The Spanish Inquisition*, Norton Publishing, 1972

Spanish Inquisition, *Encyclopedia Britannica*, 1972

Hugh Trevor-Roper, *Limpieza*, Thames & Hudson, 1970

CPSIA information can be obtained at www.ICGtesting.com
Printed in the USA
BVOW071143030513

319812BV00001B/6/A